Beyond Reality Series
Book 3

By Susan Stoker

Diane-
Thank you for
being a loyal reader! :)
Susan Stoker

Working as a camera operator for a hard-nosed producer isn't all fun and games. Kina is seriously thinking about making this reality show her last. She's known as being 'cold-as-ice' when it comes to men, which is appropriate since they're filming in Alaska. Before she can figure out what she wants to do with her life she had to make it through this show. The contestants aren't exactly lumberjack material and the challenges range from ridiculous to downright dangerous.

The Alaskan reality show is Jonathan's last gig before he goes to work in security with his brother. The shoot would be completely miserable except for the fact that the one woman in the world who is meant to be his is also a camera operator on the show. He has no idea how he'll manage it, but he is determined to win her heart and convince her to move to Arizona to be with him.

Following in the footsteps of the contestants isn't a walk in the park for the camera operators. Fighting boredom and drama within the crew, hiking across glaciers, and camping in the Alaskan wilderness isn't as safe as it seems on television. An injury on the set will either bring Jonathan and Kina together, or tear them apart for good.

This is a work of fiction. Names, characters, places and incidents are either the product of the author's imagination or used fictitiously, and any resemblance to actual persons, living or dead, business establishments, events or locales is entirely coincidental.

Frozen Hearts
All rights reserved.
Copyright 2014 © Susan Stoker

ISBN-13: 978-1508427445
ISBN-10: 1508427445

Published by Beau Coup Publishing
http://beaucoupllcpublishing.com
© Kivig | Dreamstime.com - Blue Frost Background Photo

ALL RIGHTS RESERVED. This book contains material protected under International and Federal Copyright Laws and Treaties. Any unauthorized reprint or use of this material is prohibited. No part of this book may be reproduced or transmitted in any form or by any means, electronic or mechanical, including photocopying, recording, or by any information storage and retrieval system without express written permission from the author / publisher.

Alaska was cold. That was the first thing Jonathan Baker thought after walking out of the airport in Anchorage. Hell, it was September, it theoretically wasn't that cold yet, but apparently his Arizona blood wasn't used to it. He knew it was going to be a long shoot.

This was Jonathan's last job before he could go home to Arizona and start work with his brother Dean. Dean was an independent consultant and set up security for businesses and others who requested his services. He also did some pro-bono work for women who'd been stalked or who had an ex-husband or boyfriend who wouldn't leave them alone.

Jonathan couldn't wait. He loved his brother and his family. He was thrilled Dean and Becky had finally ended up together after the fiasco of a reality show Jonathan had just filmed. The producer, Eddie, was good at his job, but he tended to only see money signs when dreaming up different ways to put 'normal' people on television. It had backfired on him in Arizona because he hadn't done his homework when choosing the contestants. Two of the men who'd been voted off the show had hurt Becky in retaliation.

Luckily, they were too drunk to do any lasting harm, although they'd beaten the crap out of her. As a result of the entire thing, after the lawyers got involved, it was determined that Eddie wasn't allowed to even air the reality show Becky had been on. Jonathan knew both his sister-in-law and brother were relieved not to have to deal with the publicity and any mental issues that might be triggered in Becky by watching the show and re-living the events.

Jonathan was just thrilled his brother had found his *One* in Becky. Throughout their family history, the men in their family found they had one woman in the world who was meant for them. Finding her was never easy, but as soon as they met her, they knew. No one understood it, but they'd heard story after story of it happening. Becky was Dean's *One*. He'd taken one look at her and known. Of course she was on a reality show to find love and Dean wasn't a contestant, so it took a bit of time, but eventually everything had worked out.

They'd gotten married in a small but very emotional ceremony at the family's animal refuge. Becky had wanted to just elope to Vegas and do it there, but Dean wanted to give her a proper wedding, even if it was small and low-key.

Jonathan loved Becky and was thrilled to have her as a part of their family. She was great for Dean and she loved the family and the animal refuge his parents owned and operated in Arizona. Jonathan was still trying to get over what he perceived as his role in her ordeal, but thank goodness she'd put the incident mostly behind her. He only wished he could put it behind him as easily.

It was only a matter of time before Jonathan could get back to the warm weather of Arizona and his new career, but he had this one last job to complete as a camera operator on the reality show to finish first. Since Eddie's last production hadn't worked out, he'd completely changed the theme of his current reality show. He'd apparently had enough of trying to hook people up and decided to go with a 'tough man' theme. This show in Alaska was about men trying to compete with each other to be crowned the one and only 'Extreme Alaskan.'

It was quite a change from the man's previous shows and Jonathan wasn't sure Eddie could pull it off. It seemed to Jonathan that there were a lot of additional safety factors that would have to be taken into account and he wasn't sure Eddie had even thought about them. If the men on the show were going to have to survive extreme Alaskan conditions, he hoped Eddie had made all of the contestants sign a liability waiver. Maybe he'd learned his lesson after the Arizona show.

Jonathan was one of a handful of camera operators. The number of crew had been reduced drastically for this show. Eddie said this was because it wasn't necessary to film the contestants back at the house they'd rented as men typically didn't have as much drama as women when they were cooped up together. Besides, Eddie had said he didn't really care if they did have drama, he was going to concentrate on filming their extreme challenges and not their antics back at the house. Jonathan figured Eddie was also probably trying to save money. He'd lost a ton of it since he hadn't been able to air his last show, so fewer camera operators equaled less money spent here in Alaska. Cheapskate.

Jonathan was looking forward to this job more than ever, because it was his last one behind the camera. This wasn't what he wanted to do with the rest of his life, and thanks to Dean, he was going to get a chance to do something different. He was also excited about this job because he'd be spending time with Kina, another camera operator. Kina was his *One*. She'd been filming on the last show in Arizona. Jonathan hadn't truly met her until the end of the show, when he'd gone to the other camera operators for help when Becky had been hurt. Kina was standoffish and somewhat rude to most everyone, but the first time he spoke to her, he knew. She was his. Somehow, some way, he'd have to make her see it.

* * *

Kina Venable shook her head. Eddie was an idiot. She had no idea why they had to film this stupid show in the wilds of Alaska, but once Eddie got something in his head, no one could change his mind. She'd been working with Eddie for a while now, as part of his crew in Australia and on the show they'd just finished in Arizona. She'd pretty much decided this would be the last time she worked for him, though. He wasn't very savvy when it came to people. Oh, he was a great producer and knew how to generate great dramatic TV, but he had no clue when it came to treating people with respect.

Kina had become good friends with Sam, one of the female contestants on the show in Australia. After the show was over, Kina had kept in touch with her. That was uncharacteristic for Kina, as she was standoffish with most people, but Sam had saved her life, and honestly, Kina liked her and wanted to get to know her better. She had spent some time visiting Sam after the last show wrapped up, needing the down-time. Seeing what'd happened to Becky had shaken her up.

She loved seeing how happy Alex and Sam were now. Eddie had tried to make sure they didn't end up together in Australia, but even editing Sam out of the reality show altogether hadn't kept the two apart.

Spending time on their ranch in Texas was always so peaceful. Sam was down-to-earth and always wanted to please everyone. Kina didn't trust many people in her life, but Sam was now one of the few people she'd trust with any secret. Something about the other woman made Kina want to open up and share her thoughts and feelings.

While she'd visited, she and Sam spent a lot of time talking about what had happened to Becky in Arizona. Kina was horrified that the men she'd gotten to know through the camera could have it in them to do something so hideous to another human being. Kina would never understand how people could do such awful things to someone else. Murderers, stalkers, rapists, pedophiles…the list went on and on. Both Kina and Sam agreed the world could be a scary place. Thank goodness Becky was all right and had Dean to lean on, now.

Kina wasn't jealous—exactly, she was happy for her friend Sam, and for Becky, but even as tough as she always acted, she wanted what they had. She hadn't had good luck finding a man who would let her be who she was, though. Because of her experiences she knew she'd become cynical and had a reputation for being a man-hater.

But for now, Kina was stuck in Alaska. As luck would have it, she was the only female camera operator on the show. Eddie had pared down the number of operators to only five. He was being really tight with money for this show. Because of all the crap that went down in Arizona he'd completely changed the premise of the show from another *'find your soul mate'* type of show, to a more extreme, *'see how macho you can be'* format. Just the sort of thing Kina hated.

She'd had enough of men acting like they were God's gift to women and behaving as if they were superior in all ways to everyone around them, especially women. Lately, she didn't like many of the guys she met. She wasn't a lesbian, although at times she thought it was a pity that she didn't swing that way. She was tired of having to have to deal with a man's crap in order to get laid. She just wanted to find a man who'd let her be who she was, but at the same time would be there for her. Her last relationship was such a disaster it almost turned her off to dating altogether. Matt had been a complete jerk. She couldn't even remember what it was that she'd liked about him in the first place.

It was ridiculous. She knew she was being unreasonable. She wanted a guy who'd let her do whatever it was she wanted to do, but yet would be as sweet to her as Alex was with Sam. Gah. She was totally messed up in the head. A man like that likely didn't exist.

Kina thought about the guys who also operated the cameras on the show. She'd worked with all of those who were contracted for this show at one time or another. Carl and Taylor, she knew from the Australian show, Jonathan, she knew from Arizona, and Jeff, she'd worked with on a past show, with a different producer.

Jeff was a jerk; she'd learned that from working with him in the past. Carl and Taylor were good men. They were both married and pulled out pictures of their kids all the time to show off, whenever they could. Carl's kids were Celeste and Catherine. And Taylor also happened to have two daughters, Phyllis and Beth. Kina loved listening to them try to outdo each other when telling stories about how cute their daughters were. Their stories were always hilarious, and of course, their kids were adorable.

Jonathan was altogether different. He made her nervous. She couldn't put her finger on why, he just did. Not nervous as in she was scared he'd hurt her, just nervous as in jittery. He was single, always polite, and she liked the way he went out of his way to help Becky when the assholes on the last show had hurt her, but there was just something about him that threw her for a loop.

He was way too good-looking, for one thing. Not many men could pull off long hair and not look like a seventies biker dude, but he managed it. His black hair was thick and went down to about the middle of his back. He usually wore it pulled back in a ponytail so it didn't get in his way while he was working. His main outfit of choice was faded jeans and a tight shirt. They were mostly short-sleeved when they had filmed in Arizona, but up here in Alaska, they were long-sleeved.

Kina never saw him lose his cool. Ever. He was the most even-keeled person she'd ever met, besides herself, and that freaked her out. It was her experience that people, especially men, were hot-headed and impulsive. Even Taylor and Carl got upset at Eddie, the contestants, each other, her…but not Jonathan.

Kina always tried to be honest with herself, but it was hard to admit that she admired Jonathan and might even like him. She typically didn't like men. But somehow, something, wouldn't let her dismiss Jonathan as easily as she had other men in the past. She admired him. That was what made him different from the other men she'd known. He was tenacious and had made sure he'd gotten all of the camera operators to talk to the police in Arizona to help Becky and he wasn't even in love with her. That kind of loyalty and compassion was rare in Kina's life and watching it made her crave that for herself. What would it feel like to have someone feel that way about her? To have that loyalty to her? It was something she'd never had, but now that she'd seen it firsthand, she wanted it to the bottom of her soul.

There was no way she'd do anything about it however, she'd just have to make it through the next six weeks until this show was over. Unless Eddie changed drastically, she'd find another production company to join up with and be on her way.

Chapter 2

Eddie gathered his camera operators around him for their first production meeting before the contestants were to arrive later that day.

"Hello again, everyone. Welcome to Alaska. I wanted to make sure you knew what I expected of you for this shoot and what the general plan is for the show. As you know, this is *not* a dating show. I'm bringing in twelve men to compete in typical Alaskan challenges each week. At the end of the six weeks, there will be two men left and they will have to go out in the wild and survive over a three day period. The person who completes all of the tasks the best will be named the ultimate *Extreme Alaskan.*

"The plan for the first few weeks is to travel only a short distance away from Anchorage to compete in mini-challenges. While those challenges are going on, you'll all have to be on hand for filming. When we aren't filming challenges, your time will mostly be your own, as will the contestants'. They won't be allowed to leave the production house, but neither will we be filming them all day, every day, either.

"Generally, you'll all be working at the same time. You won't be assigned to work all day every day, but it'll vary with what is going on each day, as to how long you'll work. I've procured a different hotel than where you stayed last night. This one is closer to the production house. You'll stay there for the rest of the shoot. I expect you to arrive at the set on time and to work your entire shift. There's a rental SUV that you'll have to share. You pay for your own gas if you decide to go anywhere other than the set and the hotel. It's up to the five of you to figure out who's driving when and where. I don't have time to deal with that crap. Also, I've had enough drama to last me a lifetime, so keep it to yourselves. I don't want to hear about it. Nothing can go wrong on this show, and I mean *nothing*. The rest of my career depends on this show going off without a hitch. Does anyone have any issues with anything I've said so far?"

Nobody said a word. Even Jeff, who was usually a complete smartass, kept his mouth shut. It was obvious Eddie was dead serious and that his past legal troubles had changed the type of producer he was.

"Great," Eddie said, continuing with his rules for the show. "When we get down to the last few challenges they'll most likely be overnight wilderness trips. You'll be split up and will be paired together to watch and film the men competing in and completing the challenges. The contestants will be sent out either in pairs or in a trio and there will be two cameras on them the entire time. I expect you to work together amicably and to get the money shots while they're out there. If you don't think you can hack the temperatures or the kind of terrain we'll be sending the contestants out in, let me know now and I'll replace you."

Kina scowled at Eddie, as he stared right at her. She glared back. Just because she was female didn't mean she couldn't handle the cold temperatures. What a jerk. When she didn't say anything, Eddie finally nodded his head and continued.

"All the contestants have signed waivers of liability so if anything happens to them on the set, anything at all, no one can come back and sue us. You're all covered as well because of the contract you signed. If you get hurt, you're covered by the company's insurance." Left unsaid, was the implication that the show would be aired no matter what might happen to a contestant or one of the camera operators as well.

"Great. Well, if you have no questions, I'll meet you all back at the production house at three this afternoon where you'll meet the men and we can get this show started."

At no time did Eddie thank them for their time or for their service. They were employees, no more and no less.

Kina watched as Eddie threw a set of keys to Taylor. He caught them midair and turned to the rest of them with a smirk. "Who's driving?" he asked unnecessarily.

They all agreed that Taylor could be the designated driver for now. He was the oldest and no one had any issues with him driving them around.

They all checked into the hotel and found their rooms were on the same floor, clustered together at the end of a hallway. It wasn't the fanciest place to stay in Anchorage, but it wasn't a dump either. Kina was actually a bit surprised. With the money problems Eddie and the production company had, she figured they'd be put up in a 'rent by the hour' kind of place. Kina noticed her room was right next to Jonathan's. She tried to ignore the tingles in her stomach at the thought of him being that close, but deep down, she was pleased.

* * *

Jonathan had listened to Eddie's words with only half an ear. He was standing by Kina and trying not to watch her as they all listened to the producer. She was beautiful. Not very tall, but all muscle. The top of her head came up to about his shoulder. She might be small, but he knew she was strong as hell. He'd watched her lug her camera equipment all over the set in Arizona and knew firsthand how heavy it was. She was no-nonsense and he admired the hell out of her for agreeing to film here. Alaska in September and October wasn't a walk in the park. After learning they'd all have to be trekking along with the contestants and roughing it just as they were, he was even more impressed. He didn't think she'd back out of the challenge and he was right.

He did have to tamp down his desire to speak up and tell her she shouldn't do it. He knew it wouldn't be safe. He saw how she'd glared at Eddie, when the man had dared to look at her when he was telling them to let him know if anyone didn't think they could handle the filming schedule and atmosphere. She wouldn't hesitate to put him in his place if Jonathan piped up and said anything to her.

Eddie had a lot to prove, so he knew the challenges and situations the contestants would be put in would be extreme. And if the men were doing extreme things, the camera operators would have to be as well, because they had to get it all on film. It wasn't as if he didn't think Kina could do the things they'd be asked to do, he just didn't want her to get hurt or even be uncomfortable. He was smart enough to keep his mouth shut, though. Kina would hate him for sure, if he even for a second, insinuated she shouldn't do it.

He was thrilled beyond words, to be right next door

to her in the hotel, even though their rooms didn't have connecting doors. Just being close to her made him feel more relaxed. It was silly, she was a grown woman and had been taking care of herself for her entire life, but he felt reassured just the same. Of course the other camera operators were also nearby. That didn't sit as well with him, but Jonathan tried to reassure himself that Carl and Taylor were happily married. He didn't know Jeff at all, but would give him the benefit of the doubt, for now.

In about three hours, it'd be time to get to the set and start setting up for their first shoot. This was always an exciting time for the contestants and camera operators alike. The time for planning was over. The show was about to start.

Because this program wasn't a dating show, Eddie had ditched his previous host, Robert. But since he knew he had to market the show to both men and women, he'd hired a woman named Shannel to be the host of this new reality show. Shannel was tall, slender, and of course, beautiful. She had an innate grace about her. Kina wanted to hate her at first glance, both because of the woman's looks and her own experiences with the previous beautiful women on Eddie's shows, but unfortunately she couldn't. Shannel was a riot. She swore like a sailor and had a wicked sense of humor. It was really hard to dislike her when the first words out of her mouth when she met all the camera operators were, "Thank you for all the hard work you do."

Jonathan, Kina, and the other camera operators got to work setting up their equipment so they'd be ready when Eddie started the show. Jonathan watched Jeff sidle up to Kina and start flirting with her. He really wasn't surprised when she ignored him and continued getting her camera ready to go. Jonathan heard Jeff mumble, "Dyke" as he walked away toward his own camera. Jonathan just shook his head. Why did guys do that? If they couldn't score with a woman they automatically accused her of being a lesbian. Ridiculous.

When the time came to set up their places for

filming, Jonathan made sure he was between Kina and Jeff. There was no use even pretending he wanted Jeff anywhere near her. He mentally shrugged as Eddie introduced the contestants.

Most of the men were tall and all were muscular. Jonathan thought they'd all have some outdoor experience, or at least some sort of survivalist job, but Eddie was smarter than that. He knew there were already shows on television about extreme survivalists competing against one another. Eddie had chosen strong muscular men, but ones with regular jobs.

Jonathan knew he'd never keep them straight, but then again, he didn't really have to. His job was to film them, regardless of who they were. As long as he had good camera angles and got all their actions on film, nothing else mattered.

Kina was fascinated with the group of men Eddie had picked for his show. The men were all good-looking and from all walks of life. Slade was a lawyer, Julio designed websites, Trent was a nurse, Zach worked in IT, Ian owned his own restaurant, Benedict was a licensed sex therapist, Drew was a probation officer, Nash wrote articles for a newspaper, Cole was a security officer, Grant was a radiologist, Roger a teacher and last, was Darius, a chemist.

It was an eclectic mix of people and jobs, and most likely personalities. Eddie might claim to not want drama and to believe that there wouldn't be any at the production house, but Kina knew he was wrong. Sometimes men could provide more drama than their female counterparts, they were usually more subtle about it, though. At the very least the competition itself would cause the men to have some disagreements.

Kina worked in tandem with the other camera

operators to get close-ups of the contestants and to get good angles of Shannel meeting each man and introducing the premise of the show. Everyone seemed eager to get started. The first challenge would be the next morning. Two men would be sent home then. Eddie's general plan was to send two men home each time they had a competition. Kina could tell the contestants were nervous, but excited at the same time.

The ride back to the hotel was filled with good humor. Everyone on the crew was in good spirits and was excited to get the show started. When they arrived back at the hotel, everyone piled out and headed toward their rooms. Jonathan watched as Kina unlocked her door and stepped inside. He made sure the door shut securely behind her and turned to glare at Jeff, who'd been watching Kina from his door as well. The other man gave Jonathan a chin lift and closed his door.

Jonathan took a deep breath. Should he or shouldn't he? It was killing him to let Kina be, knowing she was his, but he didn't have a choice. He couldn't very well invite himself into her room and settle in, no matter if he really wanted to do so. He'd barely spoken with her and he knew she was very closed-off. He didn't want to do anything to turn her against him before she really got to know him. He'd just have to wait. It wasn't what he wanted to do, but for now he'd do it.

The camera crew had arranged to meet at the car early the next morning so they could get to the set on time and be ready to go when Eddie assembled the contestants. Jonathan subtly arranged to sit next to Kina in the far back seat.

"Good morning, Kina."

"Good morning, Jonathan."

"Did you sleep well?"

"Yes, you?"

"Not really."

Kina looked directly at him for the first time that morning, her eyebrows raised. Jonathan answered her unasked question.

"I never sleep well the first night in a strange place." He debated what he wanted to say next and decided to go ahead and tell her something personal about himself in the hope she'd want to get to know him better. "I also sometimes have nightmares, so I generally don't sleep well anywhere."

Whoa. Kina wasn't sure what to say to that. She desperately wanted to know more about the handsome man sitting next to her, but she didn't want to be nosey. She knew she had a reputation of being standoffish, but she didn't want to be with this man. Aw, the hell with it. He'd brought it up in the first place.

"Nightmares?"

"Yeah, nothing I want to go into here and now, but if you get to know me better I'll share."

Kina blushed. Shit. She hadn't meant to lead him on in any way. She never did with any man, but he took her words the wrong way. She tried to backpedal. "I didn't mean…"

Jonathan interrupted her. "It's okay. I want to get to know you better and I want you to get to know me better. I probably shouldn't have thrown that out there, knowing we didn't have the time, or the privacy, to talk." He looked her in the eyes and lowered his voice, knowing the others in the car were probably listening. "I like you, Kina." He laid it on the line.

Kina blushed again. Double shit. She liked what she knew of him too, but didn't want to encourage him. Things with guys never worked out with her. Ever. Even if she wanted them to. She had to protect herself.

"Well, I don't think I like you, Jonathan." She turned away from him and focused on the scenery.

Jonathan laughed. Kina fumed. How dare he laugh! He was supposed to get pissed at her, any other normal man would. She didn't understand him at all.

Neither of them said anything else all the way to the set. When they arrived Kina immediately got busy with her equipment and tried to ignore Jonathan altogether. She didn't miss it when he stepped in front of Jeff and blocked him from setting his gear down next to hers. Interesting. She appreciated that more than she could say, but she'd never tell him. Jeff was a pain in her butt. She was constantly rebuffing him, but it never seemed to make any difference. He was like an annoying little puppy, no matter how often you scolded him, he always came back for more.

Eddie had obviously briefed Shannel about the day's activities because the hostess gathered the contestants together once the cameras were up and running to explain how the day would go. Everyone was invited into the dining room at the house where the long table was set with twelve place settings, one for each contestant. The men were instructed to each stand behind one of the chairs around the table. Once everyone was in place Shannel explained the first challenge.

"I hope you all like to eat! A big part of survival in Alaska is being able to find enough to eat. As you know, Alaska is home to a booming fishing and seafood industry. Many people make their way up to our fiftieth state to make a living off the abundance of seafood in our rivers and seas. Today, your challenge is courtesy of *Humpy's Great Alaskan Alehouse* right here in

Anchorage. It's called the Six Pound Seafood challenge. Yes, you heard me correctly. Your challenge today is to eat six pounds of seafood as fast as you can. The restaurant has their own name for this, they call it the Kodiak Arrest Challenge. For our challenge today, the two men who finish their six pounds the slowest will be leaving the show and won't have the chance to be crowned Extreme Alaskan. If there are more than two people who can't finish all their food, we will weigh whatever is left to see who'll be leaving. In this case, the two men who've eaten the lowest number of pounds of food will be going home.

"On the menu today are three pounds of luscious King Crab legs, a one-and-a-half-foot-long fresh reindeer sausage, seven salmon cakes, mashed potatoes, mixed vegetables, and for dessert, one berry crisp. You have no time limit to eat everything, but remember, the two people who finish the slowest and eat the least amount of food will be leaving. Does anyone have any questions?"

Kina laughed silently as she looked through her camera lens and saw the looks of dismay on most of the men's faces. Six pounds was a lot of food, especially considering they hadn't been warned about the food challenge. They'd most likely eaten a large breakfast to prepare themselves for the day.

The men all sat down and their plates were loaded up with the platters of food from the servers at *Humpy's*. This was great publicity for the small ale house and they'd donated the food for free. Again, Kina thought Eddie could be a jerk, but he definitely knew his business.

As the bell rang for the contest to start, the cameras rotated around the table. Every slurp, every burp, and every bite of food was immortalized on camera for the world to see. Kina wondered for the millionth time why anyone ever agreed to be on one of these shows. If only they could see what she saw through her lens. Oh, Kina knew much of it would be edited out, but it was still disgusting. She never wanted to see herself on the big screen. She was perfectly happy in the background.

After about thirty five minutes Nash was the first one finished with his plate of food. He triumphantly raised his arms and declared himself, “Done!”

Kina nearly snorted out loud. She wasn’t sure that finishing all that food first was something to crow about.

Shannel agreed that he’d finished and he was escorted to a platform behind the table to wait for the others to finish. Slowly, some of the others finished their portions. Darius, Roger, Cole, and Grant were the next four to finish. They joined Nash on the platform. There were seven men still eating. Finally, after ten more minutes, Slade and Julio joined the others. Now there were only five men left. It didn’t look like any of them were going to be able to finish all the food on their plates.

When they’d all finally given up, Shannel motioned for the scales to be brought in so they could see who ate the least.

From the camera’s perspective it was disgusting. The leftover food for each man was piled together in a bowl and placed on the scale. Kina made sure to get some good close-up shots of the uneaten food dripping down the side of the bowls. Yuck.

After all the weighing was done, Shannel gathered all the men in a room next to the dining room. They lined up and Kina barely paid attention as Shannel did a run-through of the contest. The hostess asked some of the men to discuss their strategy and to talk about what the hardest part of the competition was. When all was said and done Shannel dramatically announced that Zach and Drew had eaten the least and were declared the losers.

Kina followed Drew as he went up the stairs to pack, as Taylor followed Zach. The two men didn't say much, at least nothing that was dramatic enough to make it into the edited version of the show. The two men were escorted out of the building, with Kina and Taylor hot on their heels filming every aspect of their departure.

Meanwhile, back in the decision room, Jeff, Carl, and Jonathan filmed as Shannel told the remaining ten contestants to get some rest because the competitions would only get more difficult as time went on. She explained that the last two men standing should expect to spend a couple of nights out in the wilderness to complete challenges to determine who would be deemed the Extreme Alaskan.

* * *

Jonathan watched as Kina laid her head back on the seat in the car as they all headed back to the hotel. His fingers actually twitched to take her head in his hands and give her a massage to try to help her get rid of her headache. He didn't think she'd appreciate his familiarity. He knew she noticed that once again, he blocked Jeff's attempts to sit next to her in the car, but he didn't care. As far as he was concerned this was assigned seating and he'd always get to sit next to Kina.

"How about we all get together and have a beer at the bar?" Carl asked as they neared the hotel.

"Sounds good to me," Jeff and Taylor agreed.

Jonathan looked at Kina, waiting to see what she wanted to do. When she didn't say anything he nudged her with his shoulder. "What do you say?"

Kina opened her eyes to look at Jonathan with surprise. "Oh, me too?"

"Hell yeah, why wouldn't you think you were invited?" Carl said with surprise from the front seat.

"Well, I just figured you'd want to hang out with the guys." Kina said honestly.

"You *are* one of the guys, Kina," Carl said laughing.

Kina heard Jonathan say under his breath, "The hell she is."

She looked toward him only to see a look of innocence on his face. She laughed out loud. He was too much. "Okay, I'm in."

Jonathan smiled back at her and agreed to meet them in the hotel bar as well.

Kina looked around at the men surrounding her at the table. They all had frosty mugs of beer in front of them and were recounting the day's challenge and laughing. She was relaxed for the first time in a long time. She found she really enjoyed having a smaller group of camera operators on the set. It made for a more family-type atmosphere, something she hadn't even known she'd like.

She didn't even care that she had a headache. It wasn't awful and it was better to be here hanging out with Jonathan than sitting alone in her room again. Yes, she could finally admit it to herself. She wanted to get to know him. He fascinated her. He seemed like such a good guy and she was attracted to him. He wasn't really her type, but he was funny and courteous and had a bit of mystery about him. The attention he paid her was also very flattering and she found him very hard to resist.

She was so relaxed and mellow with the good company and good beer that she missed seeing the burly local man saunter up to their table. The first inkling she got that he was there was when she actually felt Jonathan tense at her side.

"Hey, sweet cheeks, can I buy you a beer?"

Kina looked down at the still half-full beer mug sitting in front of her. This guy had a lot of nerve, coming up to their table when she was sitting with four other men.

"Uh, no. I'm good," she told the man easily.

He obviously wasn't adept at taking no for an answer, as she'd found most men weren't, and asked again, in a voice that wasn't really a question.

"I'll buy you a beer."

Before Kina could say anything in return Jonathan had stood up and was chest to chest with the man. Words were said between them, too low for Kina to hear. The man turned around and left without a word and Jonathan sat back down. Kina immediately was pissed. What the hell?

"What the hell was that?" she asked nastily.

"I just let him know that you weren't interested." Jonathan answered calmly, taking a sip of his beer.

Kina saw red. Matt used to do the same thing all the time. Make every decision for her and not take into account what she wanted. She wasn't going there again, no way.

"How do you know I wasn't interested? Maybe I would've liked to have had a drink with him? You don't know anything about me and you don't own me.

Understand?"

Jonathan looked at his woman evenly. He didn't understand where her attitude was coming from. He'd only been protecting her from harassment. He didn't want to think of anyone else's hands on her, but if she really wanted to have a drink with that bozo he wouldn't stand in her way. But he also didn't want her doing it just to make a point.

"I'm sorry, Kina. I honestly thought you'd be more comfortable hanging here with us. I didn't think you'd want to have a drink with him. If you're really interested in him I'll go and apologize." Like hell he would, but he didn't think telling her that would get him very far in his quest to win her heart.

Kina struggled to control her temper. Jonathan wasn't Matt. He wasn't trying to control her. She took a deep breath. "No, it's okay. Just don't do it again. I like to make my own decisions."

Jonathan nodded and noticed they had an audience. The other camera operators were looking on with extreme interest. He would've liked to have talked to her more about it, but knew he wouldn't get any further in front of the others. He desperately wanted some time alone with her, but didn't know how to go about it. Maybe he'd push his luck tonight and simply ask if he could talk to her alone. He didn't know if she'd go for it, but it was worth a shot. *She* was worth it.

He hoped she was ready to go. He didn't want any other trouble tonight and Kina was just too beautiful to sit in the bar any longer without attracting more attention. It looked like it was true that there were more men than women in Alaska, at least in this bar it was.

"You about ready to go?" he asked Kina, gesturing to her beer with his chin, hoping like hell she'd say yes.

He sighed in relief when Kina nodded, even though she'd rolled her eyes while doing it. They scooted out of the booth, saying their goodbyes to Taylor, Carl, and Jeff. As they walked toward their rooms, Jonathan asked, "Can I talk to you for a second?" When she hesitated and sighed, he said quickly, "I won't take much time, I swear. We can go to your room or mine, I just want to talk to you without the others hearing for a second."

Kina considered his words. She didn't want the others overhearing whatever it was that Jonathan wanted to tell her, either. It wasn't because she thought he'd tell her something bad, it was simply because on the most basic level, she wanted to be near him. As much as she didn't like his overprotective attitude, she liked *him*.

Kina nodded and decided she'd go to his room. It was a gamble, but that way she could leave whenever she wanted. It would be harder to kick Jonathan out of her room if he didn't want to go.

Jonathan opened his door and gestured her in. Kina was surprised to find his room was spotless. She'd halfway expected him to be a slob, but she admitted to herself that was because Matt hadn't bothered to clean up after himself, so she just expected all men to be that way.

Kina watched as Jonathan puttered around the room for a moment before finally settling on the chair in the corner. He looked nervous. It put her even more at ease. Had any man ever been nervous in her presence before? Nervous in a good way, not nervous because he thought she'd rip into him. She didn't think so. Most of the time they were arrogant assholes who thought she'd do whatever they wanted her to.

Jonathan took a deep breath then said baldly, repeating what he'd already said once. "I like you, Kina." He'd decided to go for it. Kina was a no-nonsense type of woman and he figured she'd appreciate his candor more than his beating around the bush. It could backfire on him, but he couldn't stand being around her and watching her flirt with other men and generally not know he had feelings about her. When she didn't say anything but only looked at him incredulously, he continued, "I know, I know, it sounds crazy, but it's true. I admire you and want to get to know you better."

Kina was floored. That was *so* not what she'd expected him to say when she agreed to come into his room. Before she thought about it she blurted out, "Are you drunk?"

He laughed. "No hon, I'm not drunk. I just wanted to get that on the table so you'd know where I'm coming from. I don't expect you to reciprocate in kind yet, but I feel like you have the right to know."

"Since when?" Kina said, still waiting for him to laugh and say, "Gotcha" as if it was all a big joke.

"Since I met you in Arizona," Jonathan answered honestly. He always wanted to tell her the truth. He didn't believe any kind of relationship could flourish if there wasn't honesty between two people.

"Wh-what?" Kina was completely floored. She knew she wasn't the type of woman to inspire thoughts of lust and the immediate "like" that Jonathan was claiming he felt for her. "I-I don't know what to say," she managed to stammer out.

"Please, don't say anything. I hope to Christ you'll give me a chance to show you I'm a good guy. Just get to know me over the next weeks and I'll prove it to you."

Kina shook her head. This was crazy, but deep down inside something unfurled in her gut. Could he be for real? She'd have to guard her heart just in case, but God, it was such a heady feeling. She didn't really think he'd want to be with her, not after hearing all about her messed up history with men.

"You're in charge here, Kina," he told her unexpectedly. "If you want to talk to me, let me know. If you want to hold my hand, take hold. If you want to kiss me, I'm all for it. But, you're in charge. I won't push my luck, but I *will* try to convince you to give me a chance. Be forewarned, hon."

Kina hadn't ever been in charge of a relationship. In all of her disastrous relationships, she'd been pursued and then subsequently dumped. Maybe that was the problem. Maybe she needed to take control of what she wanted for once. She liked that idea. The more she thought about it, the more she liked it.

"Okay, Jonathan. I'm in charge, huh?"

"Yes, ma'am," he answered, smiling, looking like he didn't know what to expect.

"Then goodnight, I'll see you in the morning." She spun and headed toward the door.

Jonathan's laugh followed her out the door.

Chapter 4

The next morning, Kina didn't know what to think about Jonathan and their conversation from the night before. She'd almost convinced herself he didn't really mean it. But when they all met to get in the car and go to the set, he walked right up to her, took hold of her hand and brought it to his lips. He gently kissed the back of her hand, all the while not breaking eye contact.

"Good morning, Kina," he murmured, and slowly let go.

Holy crap. He was intense, and hot, and she loved it. She wasn't sure why she loved it when *he* acted that way, but had hated when Matt did the same thing. She tried to remind herself that she was in charge. She wanted nothing more than to throw him down to the ground and hump him like there was no tomorrow, but unfortunately that wasn't going to happen anytime soon. She so wasn't ready for that.

She pulled her hand back. "Thought I was in charge?"

"Just saying good morning."

That grin was lethal. Kina climbed into the SUV trying to turn her thoughts to the upcoming job. She was only partially successful.

Filming for the next two days wasn't going to be very exciting. The next challenge wasn't scheduled for a while because apparently Eddie still had to set it up.

So, while he hadn't wanted to bother with a lot of filming on set, they really had nothing else to do while they were there. Besides, there would need to be *some* filming done in the house, the entire show couldn't just be about the challenges.

Kina was hyper aware of Jonathan all day. He didn't break his promise to her; he was letting her call the shots in whatever relationship they might or might not have. It was driving her crazy. She didn't know how to be in charge of a relationship and she still wasn't convinced she even wanted one with Jonathan. She couldn't deny he was hot as hell and that she was attracted to him, but… There was always a but. She wasn't good at relationships. From her high school boyfriend to Matt, that had been made clear over and over.

In order to have a good relationship, there had to be trust, and Kina certainly no longer felt she could trust anyone. Time and time again, any trust she'd given to someone had been broken.

Jonathan was having a good day. He felt relieved he'd told Kina how he felt. It would be the hardest thing he'd ever had to do, to not immediately try to plow right over any objections she might have about their relationship, but he'd promised to let her take control. And he would, even if it killed him.

* * *

The next couple of days continued much as the previous ones had. The group got up in the mornings and went to the production house where they got some random shots of the men sitting around talking, playing pool, cooking lunch, or whatever they happened to be doing. Shannel was scarce, as her job was to play host, not babysit the contestants.

Eddie had been around, mostly to direct some shots that he wanted, but he was also busy setting up the challenges that would happen in the upcoming weeks.

After filming for the day, the group would go back to the hotel and have a drink and dinner. There were no more incidents with any local men trying to hit on Kina and even Jeff was behaving himself for the moment.

Jonathan took every opportunity to brush up against Kina or to just sit next to her and listen to her talk. He thought she was loosening up around him, but he couldn't be sure. All he could do was wait for her to give him a sign, or flat out tell him she wanted to be with him.

Kina was ready to give whatever it was between her and Jonathan a try. They'd been tiptoeing around each other for a while now, and she honestly wanted to get to know him better. That night, before they met up at the hotel restaurant for dinner, Kina decided to just go for it. She'd never know what kind of man Jonathan was if she didn't do as he said, take control. If it turned out he was a jerk, she'd deal. But there was a little voice in her head asking, *'what if he's not?'* She didn't *know* his brother Dean, but after being around their parents while the last show had been filmed at their animal refuge and seeing how Dean was with Becky, she figured Jonathan might, just *might*, be worth the effort.

"Hey Jonathan, wait up."

Jonathan stopped before entering the restaurant. If Kina asked him to lie down in the middle of the road, he probably would've.

Kina stood next to Jonathan and was suddenly tongue-tied. What if he said no? Oh, the hell with it.

"Doyouwanttogosomewhereelsefordinner?" she said as fast as she could.

Inside Jonathan was doing cartwheels, but he stayed calm. "Sure. I'd love to. Got any idea what you want to eat?"

Kina shook her head. It was enough that she'd asked him if he wanted to eat with her. She hadn't thought so far in advance as to what or where she wanted to eat.

"Can I make a suggestion?" At her nod he continued, "There's a place I've read about called *The Bubbly Mermaid* downtown. I've heard they have excellent fresh seafood."

"Sounds good," Kina murmured, glad she didn't have to come up with a place to eat. She probably would've chosen a fast food restaurant or something equally lame.

"Let me go and see if Taylor has the keys on him. I'll be right back." Jonathan quickly squeezed her elbow before heading into the restaurant to find the other camera operator.

While waiting for Jonathan to come back out, Kina leaned against the wall in the hallway. He'd acted perfectly with her. He didn't make a big deal out of her asking him to dinner. He could've been an ass about the whole thing, but he hadn't. She saw Jeff walking toward her. She smiled at him and said hello. His response stunned her.

"So, you finally made your move, huh? When you're done with him, I'd love a go."

Kina was stunned into silence for a moment, then what he said finally penetrated.

"What the hell, Jeff? You're an ass. It'll be a cold day in Hell before you get a 'go'."

She was going to say more when Jeff was suddenly flying backward. Jonathan had come back and grabbed Jeff by the collar of his shirt and flung him around. Jeff hit the wall on the other side of the hallway, but was able to regain his balance so he didn't fall.

"You heard her. Kiss off, Jeff. She's not going anywhere with you. She's mine. And if you so much as look cross-eyed at her again, you'll have me to deal with."

Kina was shocked to realize Jonathan was really pissed. He'd always been so mild-mannered and polite. She hadn't even realized he had it in him. She should be upset, seeing how Matt always got so jealous when she even so much as looked at another guy, but this was somehow different. He was standing up for her, not acting irrationally. He hadn't beaten the hell out of Jeff, which said a lot about his control. Besides she would've done the same thing if she'd been strong enough.

"Whatever, dude, she's not worth it." Jeff tried to recover.

"That's where you're wrong and why you'll never have anything as precious as her in your life. Keep movin'." Jonathan shot back as he took Kina's elbow in his large hand and steered her toward the door, making sure to keep his own body between hers and Jeff's. He walked them out and didn't say another word until he was opening the passenger door of the SUV for Kina.

"Are you okay?"

"Yeah, sure." Kina said, amazed that it was actually true. She was good. While she'd never be completely comfortable with someone sticking up for her when she could do it herself, it felt good to have Jonathan stick up for her.

"He's a dick," Jonathan responded more to himself

than to Kina.

Kina laughed. It felt good to release some of her tension. "Yup, he is."

Jonathan laughed as well and after she'd sat down in the front passenger seat, he pulled the belt of her seatbelt out and held it for her. Kina looked up at him as he stood there waiting for her to buckle herself in. No one had ever done that before. Oh, she'd had dates open her door, but never had someone pulled her belt out for her and handed it to her. It was sexy as hell. She took the belt from his hand and his fingers brushed against hers in the process. She shivered. God, he felt good.

Jonathan walked around the front of the SUV, trying to get himself back under control. His adrenaline was sky high. First, because of Jeff. He wanted to pummel him into the ground for disrespecting Kina. Now, because of the slight touch of her fingers against his. He was in big trouble if that was all it took for him to get excited around her. He'd never survive a kiss or anything more.

The drive to *The Bubbly Mermaid* was done in silence, but not an uncomfortable one. Kina relaxed into the seat. That was another thing different about Jonathan. He never felt the need to fill the air with unnecessary conversation. Again, he was very purposeful. He spoke when he had something to say and acted when it was necessary. Otherwise, he was content to just watch or listen.

When they pulled up to the restaurant and parked, Jonathan turned to Kina.

"Do I need to apologize for what happened back there?"

Kina knew he was referring to his actions with Jeff. "No." At the relieved look on his face Kina continued quickly. "As long as you don't make it a habit of knocking around men that talk to me. I hear a lot of crap, being a woman in this job. I can deal with it."

Jonathan took a deep breath and thought about how he could say what he needed to say and not piss her off. He held his hand out, hoping she'd put her own in his. When she slowly placed her hand in his, Jonathan was thrilled. He lightly wrapped his hand around hers and rubbed it with his thumb. "Kina, I'll do my best, but as long as I'm around, no one is allowed to be disrespectful to you. I can't just stand there and let them get away with it. I'll try to curb my reactions, but you don't have to deal with that crap by yourself anymore. I have your back."

Kina just looked at him. Was he for real? She couldn't remember a time in her life when someone 'had her back'. It had always been just her. She couldn't process this right now. She'd have to think about it later, so she just nodded.

Jonathan smiled, squeezed her hand, and told her to stay put. He hopped out his side of the vehicle, walked around to open her door, and help her out. As they walked toward the front door of the quirky restaurant, Kina decided to go for it and reached for his hand and twined her fingers with his. His large calloused hand wrapped around her smaller one felt so good. She looked up at him and he smiled down at her. That smile was worth any angst she'd had about taking his hand.

They were shown to a booth in the back of the restaurant and Jonathan gestured her into one side of the booth and when she was scooting in asked if he could sit on her side. Shocked, she could only agree. Again, that was something no date had ever asked before. They'd always sat across from her. Always. Even Matt did that when he'd take her out. Of course, after they'd been dating for a while, it had happened less and less.

The restaurant had a large selection of oysters, but Kina didn't care much for them. She was more of a shrimp and crab girl. She ordered the King Crab cocktail and Jonathan ordered seafood chowder and a plate of Alaska oysters fresh from Halibut Cove and Kachemak Bay.

Now that they'd ordered and were settled, Jonathan turned to Kina.

"So, tell me about yourself."

Kina laughed. "That sounds like a cheesy pick-up line," she told him unabashedly.

He chuckled back at her. "I suppose it did, but I want to know about you, Kina. I want to know everything about you."

Kina sobered. "That's a pretty tall order," she said seriously, having no idea where to start.

"What if we play a game? You can ask me anything and I promise to answer honestly, and then I get to ask you a question. We'll continue until you want to stop. Remember, you're in charge here."

Kina laughed, "Yeah right. I don't think I've been in charge from day one."

They both smiled.

"Okay, you're on. I get to go first, though," Kina told him, picking up her glass and taking a drink of water, while watching him nod.

"Let's see….is this like truth-or-dare where if you don't like what I ask you have to do something crazy to get out of answering?"

Jonathan didn't even smile. "No, hon. If I feel like I can't answer you honestly, I'll let you know. If I'm uncomfortable with the question, I'll answer what I can, but I'll tell you that I don't want to answer it right now. I promise, however…" He paused and took a sip of his own water as if he was nervous, before continuing, "…I'll answer your question at some point while we're here in Alaska. I want you to trust me and it might be too early for you to hear all my answers at this point."

God. Kina loved that answer.

"I don't know if I can trust you," she blurted out without thinking.

"I know." Jonathan answered immediately, not looking surprised or upset in the least. "I can tell it's hard for you to trust people and that's okay. I'm perfectly happy with you taking your time. I want to know everything about you and all about who made it so hard for you to put your trust in someone. But I'd rather have your honest and complete trust whenever you decide you can give it to me, than force you to lie to me now and say something when it's not true."

Seriously, everything that came out of his mouth just got better and better. Was he for real? All right, she had to think of some good questions to ask him.

"Okay, wow. Hmm. Let's see. I'll start out easy. What's your favorite color?" She wanted to start out simple to break the intensity in the conversation.

"That's easy. Blue. My turn."

Kina squirmed in her seat. It seemed like a good idea when *she* was the one that got to ask the questions. It wasn't as much fun being on the other side.

"Are your toenails currently painted?"

Huh? That was his question? "That's your question?" she repeated what she was thinking incredulously.

"Yup. I've been imagining what your delicate feet look like for days. And thinking about your cute little feet led me to think about your toes. Then I got to wondering if you were the type of woman who liked to paint her toenails a sexy red or maybe with a sheer coat of pink…believe me, I've spent a lot of time imagining what you look like with naked…feet."

Kina blushed hotly. Jesus. She squirmed in her seat. He was good. "Uh, no. Just plain toenails. No color," she squeaked out.

Jonathan picked up her hand and ran his thumb idly over the back of it. She was so cute. This was fun. "Your turn again, honey."

"Uh yeah, okay. Um. I heard you telling Carl this was your last job as a camera operator. Why?"

He answered without hesitation, hiding nothing from her. "I hate it." At her raised eyebrows and obvious shock he continued, "I've been living in Los Angeles for the last few years and the people there are so fake and jaded. I thought maybe filming for reality shows would be better, but it's not. I've had enough. My brother Dean, you met him on the last show, is going to let me come and work with him. I'll be able to be near him and Becky, as well as my folks. I can't wait. I've missed my family."

Wow, Kina would love to have a place she could call home. She'd never really thought about it. All she'd known for the last few years was moving from one set to another. But to have a place where you belonged, where you could put down roots was something she'd always wanted, but hadn't been able to hold on to.

"Tell me how you got into this occupation."

Kina thought about Jonathan's question for a moment. Her answer wasn't a quick and easy one, by any stretch. How much should she tell him? She looked at the man sitting next to her quietly, waiting for whatever she wanted to tell him. She made the decision to be honest.

"A while ago I was broke and homeless. I'd just left my boyfriend and didn't have any ambition, or anywhere to go. An old acquaintance of mine felt sorry for me and let me move into the basement apartment of a house she was renting out. She also got me in touch with someone she knew in the television business who needed a daytime janitor. I started working and the cameras fascinated me. I paid attention, got friendly with the people who worked there and learned all I could. One thing led to another and here I am. I took the job with Eddie because it got me out of that crappy little town and allowed me to move around. I don't have any family and Matt had made sure I didn't have any friends, so there was nothing for me there."

She looked down at the hand Jonathan was holding and winced. He'd been squeezing it harder than was comfortable. Just as she went to pull her hand away he suddenly loosened his fingers and put them in his lap. She could see his fists were clenched. His voice, when he spoke however, was calm.

"I'm sorry you had to go through that, but I'm glad you got out of that situation and you're here now. I have about a million more questions I'd love to ask about some of what you just shared, but I hope you'll tell me when you're ready. This was supposed to be a lighthearted game so we could get to know each other better."

Kina put her hand over Jonathan's in his lap. She could feel the tension. It warmed her inside that he was trying to hide it from her. This definitely wasn't like her. In the past she would've warned him away from caring about her at all. But now. it felt right.

"I didn't mean to go there, but I'm not sorry I told you. Matt, my last boyfriend, did a number on me. I'll admit it. He tried to control everything I did. He told me what I could eat. He alienated all my friends. He made me dependent on him for everything and I hated it. I hated myself when I was with him. I can't ever go back to that sort of relationship. I don't know if I even have it in me to trust any man again after what he did."

Jonathan consciously tried to relax. Every muscle in his body was tense and he wanted to go and beat the hell out of this Matt person, but he had to keep himself in control. He knew Kina wasn't the type of person who wanted or needed that kind of man. She was independent and he loved that about her. It wouldn't be easy to tone down his protective instincts when it came to her, but he'd try. He turned his hand over and captured hers in his now relaxed grip.

"Thank you for sharing that with me. I know it wasn't easy. I swear I don't want to control you. I want to be with you. I want to stand next to you, not in front of you. If you allow me to spend time with you I'll show you that you can trust me. I won't let you down."

Kina opened her mouth to say something, she wasn't sure what, when the waiter arrived with their meal. *Saved by the food!*

Jonathan was content to let the serious subject drop for now. Kina had opened up to him and he was more than pleased. It had to mean she was beginning to trust him a little bit. He could wait.

Throughout dinner they continued their game of asking questions, although none were as intense as before.

"Which do you like better, chicken or steak?" Kina asked.

"Steak. What's your favorite scent?"

"Hyacinths. They smell so good! If you could be any animal what would you be?"

"Hippo."

Kina laughed at his answer, not expecting it. "Hippo? Who chooses that? Why a hippo?"

"No one messes with a hippo. Think about it. If you saw a hippo, what would you do? I'll tell you, you'd run the other way." Kina had to agree. God, he was hysterical. It was his turn.

"What's the most embarrassing thing you've ever done?"

"If I told you, I'd just be embarrassed all over again!" They both laughed.

He let it slide and asked another question instead. "What do you think of men with long hair?"

"Easy," Kina said easily reaching over to finger the end of the long pony tail hanging down his back. "I never thought I'd like it, but now I think it's sexy as hell."

Jonathan almost spit the water he'd been drinking across the table. Good God. He was hoping for a positive answer, but that was way more than he could've hoped for. He smiled at her, changing the subject to keep himself from kissing the hell out of her. "Your turn."

Their questions eventually turned into a game Jonathan used to play with his brother all the time. They called it, 'Would you rather.' He thought he remembered reading somewhere that it'd been made into an actual game people could buy, but he could only remember the fun times he'd had with his family playing it. The object was to pick one of two equally horrible choices. It was hilarious and Kina got into the spirit of the game without hesitation.

"Would you rather be bald or excessively hairy?"

"Would you rather break an arm or a leg?"

"Would you rather eat breakfast foods for the rest of your life or only dinner foods?"

They sat laughing and talking until they finally noticed they were the only people left in the restaurant. They'd been there for hours and Kina couldn't remember having a better time with anyone in her entire life. Jonathan was fun to be around and she felt no pressure. He was being true to his word and letting her set the pace of their relationship.

They apologized to the manager for staying so long, paid their bill and made their way to the SUV. It was late and it was dark. Kina felt Jonathan's hand at the small of her back as he steered her toward their parking spot. She noticed him constantly scanning the area as if looking for trouble. He didn't run to the car, but he also didn't waste any time. He was protecting her, and she couldn't get upset with him. When Matt used to do stuff like that it annoyed the hell out of her, but she knew it was because he felt as if she belonged to him and was just looking for a reason to beat the hell out of someone. She honestly believed Jonathan was doing it because she was important to him and he wanted to make sure she was safe. She had no idea how she knew that, but she did.

Once again he opened the door for her and when she was settled into the seat he handed her the seat belt. God, why that made goose bumps break out over her body, she had no idea. Kina decided she liked it when Jonathan looked after her.

After they were on their way back to the hotel Kina asked, "Would you rather have to rollerblade everywhere you went or skateboard?" Jonathan smiled. She liked the game they had played with one another. It was intimate and personal. Hell, she just liked Jonathan.

Chapter 5

It was time for another challenge. Eddie was upping the ante with this second challenge and the men were going to have to do something a bit more physical. Their task this week was to split logs. Alaskans who didn't live in cities usually used wood stoves to heat their homes. They had to split a lot of logs to keep warm throughout the long brutal winters.

Kina laughed. She didn't think any of the contestants had ever had to split logs before. This would be funny.

The men were loaded into two separate vans along with Shannel and Eddie and some of the other producers. The camera crew took their own SUV. Eddie didn't care about having any shots of the men in the car on the way to the venue.

They drove south of the city to Chugach State Park. The Park Rangers had cleared a small section of the park for them to film in. The men were given a lesson on the safest and most efficient way to use the axe. Many times people would use a wedge to assist them in chopping, but Eddie thought that was too wimpy for the show. After donning safety glasses and gloves, each man was allowed to practice chopping one log to get the hang of it.

After safety had been taken care of, the show could start. Eddie lined all the men up and let Shannel do her hosting duties. She explained the premise of the contest, that the men each had ten minutes to chop as many logs as they could. Big trees were already chopped up into sections. Each section had to be cut up by the contestants into pieces that would fit into a typical wood stove. Each one would be measured and should be around six to eight inches in diameter. Anything larger would be thrown out.

The man who'd chopped the most legal sized pieces, the quickest, would win. The two men who chopped the least, the slowest, would be going home.

In order to save some time the men would be chopping two at a time. It was going to take probably around two hours to get through everyone as it was. Making sure camera angles were appropriate and each area was cleaned up between contestants was also important. Kina knew that when people were watching the show it would only take around ten minutes for everyone to get through their turn because of editing, but in reality it took hours because of having to re-do the set for each man. Not to mention safety procedures and questions that might arise during the filming.

Taylor and Kina were placed around one chopping area and Jonathan and Carl were set around the other. Jeff was a 'floater,' meaning he had to walk around and film the reactions of the other contestants and other interesting shots as the chopping was occurring.

The first men to go were Slade the lawyer, and Darius the chemist. They each set up at their block of wood and when Shannel blew the whistle, they were off. Darius completely missed with his first swing of the axe. Slade wasn't much better; but at least he hit the wood with his first strike, but then he couldn't get the axe out of the chunk of wood. And so it went.

Kina tried not to laugh as each group of men took their turn. It was obvious Julio, the web site developer, had never even held an axe before, because despite the instruction they'd had, he first tried to chop the chunk of wood with the blunt side of the axe. Roger and Trent were a bit better, but not by much. Kina was shocked at how good Benedict was. He'd obviously had some experience in the past, because he actually had a stack of something that resembled firewood at the end of his ten minutes.

It was during Ian's and Nash's heat that the first injury occurred. Nash was furiously trying to chop the wood as fast as he could and when he swung the axe upward to take another hit, it flew out of his hands. Kina saw it go flying right toward Jonathan. She was supposed to be watching Ian through her lens to get the best shots, but she couldn't help but see the deadly weapon flying straight toward Jonathan. Luckily, he was paying attention and stepped out of the way of the missile at the last minute. When it landed, blade first, it hit a rock and a piece came flying up and hit Carl on the side of the head.

Carl was too much of a professional to stop filming. He kept on rolling until the ten minutes was up. Kina tried to pay attention to Ian, but all she could think about was, if Jonathan hadn't stepped out of the way, he could have been hit with the axe. It was bad enough to see the trickle of blood coming from the side of Carl's face, all she could think was that it could've been Jonathan's skull bleeding.

After Eddie finally said "cut" after the time was up, Trent, a nurse, went over to Carl to see if he could help. Carl tried to blow off the whole incident, but for once Eddie was a being a stickler for safety. Everyone gathered around Carl while Trent bandaged the slight cut on the side of his head. He absolutely refused to go to the hospital and Eddie actually made him sign a piece of paper that said he refused to go.

Nash tried to apologize profusely, but Carl wasn't having it. Kina tried to get herself back into the swing of filming again, but it was hard. She didn't like to think of anyone being hurt, especially a friend like Carl, but the close call for Jonathan was never far from her mind. She knew Jonathan was trying to catch her eye, but she refused to look at him. She had to get herself together.

Finally, each of the ten contestants finished with their chopping. Shannel lined them all up again to announce the verdict. Benedict was the overall winner, which wasn't surprising to anyone. He'd done a great job. In the end Julio and Cole, the security officer, had chopped the least amount of wood. Because they weren't back at the production house, they had to 'pretend' to leave. Jeff filmed them walking toward the van and getting in. Kina knew they'd splice in a shot of the van leaving later. But for now, some of the contestants joined Julio and Cole in one van and everyone else piled in the other to go back to the house.

Kina was glad she didn't have to be in the van; the men had been sweating profusely. It wasn't actually warm outside, but the exertion of chopping the wood plus their nerves, were enough to make them quite odiferous.

Eddie told the camera operators they had the rest of the day off. Nothing was going to go on back at the house, except for Julio and Cole packing their stuff and leaving the set. Eddie had learned his lesson in Arizona and each of the men, after leaving the show, were brought to a different hotel until the end of the show.

That would assure that no one knew who won, but it was also protection for the contestants themselves in case someone didn't agree with the results of the competitions.

The camera crew piled into the SUV, ready to head back to the hotel to get their own showers. Kina leaned over the seat toward Carl.

"Are you really okay, Carl?"

"Sure, Kina, it really only winged me, not a big deal. Besides, you know I have a hard head."

Kina tried to joke with him, "Impressive you didn't drop the camera!"

Carl mock bowed and tipped an imaginary hat in her direction.

They all laughed. It actually *was* amazing he hadn't stopped filming.

Kina sat back and let the conversation and good natured ribbing continue around her. She looked over at Jonathan for the first time since they'd climbed into the car. She didn't know what she expected him to say, but she never thought he'd make light of the situation.

"Would you rather be hit by a flying axe or a flying hammer?"

She didn't want to laugh, truly she didn't, the situation wasn't funny in the least, but she couldn't help it. Damn it. Why'd he have to be funny on top of everything else?

"Ha, ha, very funny, twinkle toes." At his smile she continued. "How'd you know that thing was coming at you since you were watching only through the camera lens?"

Jeff sat sideways and put his elbow on the back of his seat. "Yeah, that was actually pretty impressive, Baker."

Jonathan waved his hand as if waving off any kind of praise. "I saw him trying to grip the handle on the few swings he took before that one. He was losing his grip on every swing; I figured it was only a matter of time. I was already planning on moving to a different vantage point when he let it fly. I guess I was just lucky."

"Damn lucky, if you ask me," Taylor called back from the front seat. Kina had to agree.

When they got back to the hotel Jonathan waited until the others had left to go up to their rooms. He lightly grasped Kina's elbow and asked. "Want to do something today?"

"I thought you were going to let me be in charge?" she told him teasingly.

Jonathan grinned. God, she was cute. "Okay, so what do you want to do for the rest of the day?"

Kina laughed. How he ever thought he'd be able to let her make all the decisions she'd never know. "What did you have in mind?" She knew he had to have something up his sleeve or he wouldn't have asked her.

"What about the Alaska Native Heritage Center?"

Kina didn't know what to say. She thought he might say the name of another restaurant or something. She never thought he'd be into something educational. She blushed. She'd stereotyped him, and she didn't like that about herself.

"Sure, sounds interesting."

As Jonathan pulled the keys out of pocket, Kina looked at him. She smirked; he'd had it planned the entire time. The rat.

As if Jonathan knew what she was thinking, he said, "I asked Taylor for them earlier. He said he didn't mind if we took the car again today. He said he was going to call home and then take a nap."

Jonathan settled Kina into the front passenger seat and once again handed her the seatbelt. Kina loved it.

When they were on the road to the Heritage Center she asked him why he'd chosen it.

"I just thought if we were going to spend six weeks in Alaska, I'd like to get to know more about the culture of the people and the history. It's fascinating to me how the Eskimos and Native people have lived for hundreds of years, doing things the same way, passed down from generation to generation. I thought we'd get an appreciation of the Native people and their traditions and history of the state."

"I'd like that." Jonathan was a lot deeper than she'd ever given him credit for. He was like an onion, the layers just kept peeling off one by one, revealing more and more of the man underneath. She was liking what she'd seen so far.

Jonathan parked the SUV and they strolled into the Center, hand in hand. Kina didn't even hesitate to grasp his hand when he held it out to her as he helped her from the car. Holding his hand was almost as natural as breathing. She didn't even try to think about how fast he'd become important to her. She just accepted it, and hoped like hell he wouldn't break her heart. He'd just started to thaw it out, she didn't want to imagine what would happen if he broke her trust now.

They walked around and checked out the different exhibits. There were a lot of fun things for kids to do. There were traditional dances that were held at the center as well, but none were being held that day. It didn't matter. They were enjoying just being with each other and learning about a different way of life and culture. Talk eventually turned to work.

"What do you think of the show?" Jonathan asked

Kina. "You were with Eddie in Australia. Do you think he's changed at all?"

Kina thought about it before answering. "Yes and no. Yes, this show is different in that Eddie isn't trying to hook anyone up. I think he learned his lesson from Arizona. But I also think he's still Eddie. He'll still try to manipulate anyone he can, in order to make the show a success. He has even more to lose now after not being able to air the Arizona show."

She paused. Not knowing if it was really appropriate to ask her next question, but she remembered what Jonathan had said at dinner, that he'd tell her the truth if he could. She figured if he didn't want to answer, he'd tell her. "Can I ask you something?"

He didn't hesitate to reassure her. "Of course hon, anything."

"How is Becky doing? I feel so horrible about what happened to her back in Arizona. I had no idea those guys would attack her at the hotel. I was in the limo when she was dropped off. I just feel like maybe I should have done something…" Her voice trailed off.

Jonathan stopped their stroll and pulled her over to a bench against a wall. They sat and he put their clasped hands on his thigh and put his other hand over the two of theirs. "She's okay, Kina. She's been seeing a therapist and working through her issues. She and Dean are so in love, it's almost sickening." He said that with a smile so she'd know he was kidding. His voice got serious again. "Remember how I told you I don't sleep well? That I get nightmares?" At her nod he continued. "It's because of what happened to her. I should have stopped it. I had every chance and I didn't."

"I don't believe that," Kina said without even

asking what he meant. “Seriously, Jonathan, I don’t know how you think you could’ve done anything, but I know without a doubt you did everything right that night. You couldn’t have done anything differently.”

Jonathan gave her a sad smile. “Thanks hon, but you don’t know…”

Before he could continue Kina interrupted him. “I *do* know. Jonathan, my God, there’s no way you’d have let anyone get hurt on your watch. You need to let this go.”

“I can’t,” he said simply.

“Have you talked to someone about this?” Kina asked him seriously. “I know most men think they’re too macho to need any help getting through horrible things that happen to them, but it sounds as if you need to talk it through.”

At his shake of his head she said boldly, “I’m here if you want to talk to me about it.”

Jonathan grasped their hands tighter and bowed his head. “I’m afraid if I tell you what happened, you’ll not want to see me anymore.”

Whoa. She hadn’t ever seen that kind of deep honest emotion from a man. Kina pulled their clasped hands up to her mouth and kissed his knuckles. “I might not know you that well, Jonathan, but I do know you’re one of the good guys. You didn’t hurt Becky. You didn’t cause her to be hurt. Some idiots did that all on their own. Hell, you won’t even let some guy say jerky things to me and you don’t even really know me. There’s no way you’d stand aside and let someone your brother loved get hurt. I’d love for you to talk to me. I’d love for you to tell me everything. If you think I’ll turn my back on you, I’ll prove you wrong. I don’t think this is the time or the place, but maybe once we get to know each other better, you'll trust me."

Jonathan's eyed glowed as he looked at her. "Believe it or not, I do trust you, Kina. I trust you more than I trust myself. I'll tell you, but you're right, not now. Will you take a rain check?"

Kina simply nodded, too choked up with emotion to talk. She'd never had a guy open himself up to her like Jonathan just had. Every boyfriend she'd ever had was a macho jerk who never really allowed her in, emotionally. She hadn't really known Jonathan that long and he'd already opened himself up more to her than anyone ever had before. She really hoped he was serious.

They continued making their way through the Heritage Center. It was an amazing place and Kina hoped one day to be able to come back and see some of the demonstrations. It was a small glimpse into a fascinating culture.

As they walked out of the building toward the car, Kina asked Jonathan, "Would you rather be stuck for five hours in an elevator or on a ski lift?" Thus began their hilarious trip back to the hotel.

Jonathan thought this was one of the most boring shoots he'd ever been on, but that actually worked in his favor with Kina, because it made her more willing to talk to him as well as giving them more time to talk to each other. Since there was no competition on the show, other than the actual contests, the men had been quite well-behaved. As much as he hated the drama of men fighting for women or men competing for a woman's attention that always happened on dating shows, at least it was interesting for the camera operators. There was always someone and something interesting to film.

This was torture. All that happened between contests was everyone sitting around. Jonathan had heard rumors that Eddie was trying to speed up production and he was all for it. The sooner they got done here, the sooner he could go home and start his new career.

The only problem with that, was Kina. He wanted more time with her. He wanted more time for her to get to know him. She was his *One*. If he didn't break through her emotional barriers before they left Alaska, he didn't know if he'd ever get a chance to. He wanted her. He wanted her more than anything he'd ever wanted in his life. All the other women he'd known paled in comparison to Kina. It wasn't just her looks, although she was beautiful to him, it was her. Her larger-than-life personality, her zest for life, and just her all-around demeanor.

He loved that she'd taken right to the silly game of 'Would you rather.' Some of the best times they'd had, had been a result of the answers and conversations they'd had over the questions they'd come up with. He didn't want to lose her. He knew he had to talk to her about what had happened in Arizona, but he was honest when he told her he was scared of losing her. Even though Becky had told him time and time again that she didn't blame him, he blamed himself. He wasn't sure he could get over it. He was trying, but it was difficult.

There were only six men left on the show. The last contest had been a few days prior. The men had been challenged to see how many fish they could catch in a net. The catch was that they were in a stream that was freezing. It wasn't like they could just stand on the bank and fish, either. No, they had to get right out in the middle of the fast-moving water and catch as many fish as possible. As far as 'extreme' went, it wasn't very, but Jonathan knew Eddie was saving the harder challenges for the upcoming competitions. Slade and Grant were the last two men to be sent packing. They'd caught the least number of fish and were currently thanking their lucky stars that they were sitting in nice warm hotel rooms, waiting out the rest of the show.

This next contest was the first one where the contestants would be 'roughing' it outside overnight, and thus, the first time the camera operators would also be roughing it. Jonathan was worried about who would be paired up. He desperately wanted Eddie to put him and Kina together, but he also didn't want Kina to think he'd put Eddie up to it. He wouldn't protest if they weren't together, only if Kina was paired with Jeff. He didn't trust Jeff as far as he could throw him. He'd been behaving after their altercation in the hallway, but he'd learned from those jerks on the Arizona show never to underestimate someone's need for revenge. No matter how pissed Kina got with him, he wouldn't allow her to spend the night out in the wilderness with Jeff.

Eddie wanted to have a meeting with all the camera crew before they were sent off. He wanted to explain the rules of the contest to everyone. He figured the camera operators could act as the 'officials' so no one would cheat.

"Here's how it's going to work. We'll be in the Chugach National Forest. There's a lake there called Eagle Lake. The men will be paired off around the lake. They shouldn't cross paths, but everyone will be in one general location. There are only five of you, so we'll split up into pairs and then there will be only one of you with one of the groups of contestants." He shrugged. "That's just the way it has to be."

When no one disagreed with him or otherwise protested, he continued.

"The men will be given basic provisions, flint, an emergency blanket, an axe, one MRE for the two of them, and one extra pair of socks. We'll set them up with some cold weather gear before they head out, jackets, long underwear, etc. They'll be expected to set up camp and be out for three days and two nights. In a few hours, we'll drop everyone off and pick them up around noon on the third day. Their task to be accomplished, will be to build a raft they'll have to actually use. When we come to pick them up they'll have to demonstrate their raft floats by paddling out three hundred yards into the lake, then turn around and come back to their campsite. Whoever builds the least water-worthy raft, or if they can't paddle the six hundred yards, will be going home. If more than one group can't make it the entire way, whichever group goes the shortest distance will be leaving.

"Your jobs, as constant observers, will be to make sure there is no cheating going on. You'll all be equipped with a radio just in case. You'll each have your own tent and provisions. No fires, though. Only the contestants are allowed to start a fire. If you light a fire the men might be tempted to use it instead of building their own. This is about them, not about you. And another thing… I don't want anyone getting hurt, is that clear? If these pussies can't handle the weather and get frostbite or if they cut off a limb, contact me immediately. If they just want to quit, too bad. They can't. That makes for great TV. People love to watch men, who think they're tough, be miserable and whiny. We haven't had enough of that on the show yet. Everyone understand?"

Jonathan shook his head. Man, Eddie was a jerk. He wondered how the man had made it this far in his career, but he supposed you had to be heartless to be a producer of reality shows.

Eddie continued. "Okay, so I've decided who will be with who."

Jonathan held his breath. He really hoped he didn't have to get all macho alpha in front of Kina.

"Jeff, you and Carl will be with Trent and Ian."

Jonathan let out his breath. Thank God. He could live with wherever Eddie put him now.

"Jonathan and Kina will be with Roger and Darius, and Taylor, you'll be by yourself with Benedict and Nash. Anyone have any problems with that? Taylor, you all right with being on your own?"

Taylor nodded, as everyone expected he would.

"Okay, you'll all be given a small tent and a sleeping bag to stay in while out there. There is, of course, no sharing those with the contestants. They have to figure out how to stay warm on their own. If you run into any situations out there, as I said, just use the radio to call back. For the next hour we'll be getting the men outfitted in their gear and you all can meet back here for Shannel to explain the contest to the men and we'll get headed out.

Jonathan was thrilled he'd be spending the next two nights with Kina. He couldn't have planned it better himself. He sensed someone coming up to stand next to him and turned to see Kina standing there, looking furious.

"What the hell?" She hissed at him. "Did you set this all up? Did you go to Eddie and tell him you were trying to get me in bed and to put us together?"

"Whoa, whoa, whoa. I didn't say anything to Eddie about us. What's happening between us is just that, between us. I'd *never* disrespect you that way."

He watched as Kina's breath heaved in and out of her chest. God, she was magnificent. He wished she hadn't immediately thought the worst of him, but he couldn't deny she was glorious when she was worked up. He tried again to soothe her when she didn't say anything. He stepped closer to her and was thrilled when she didn't take a step back. Whether she'd admit it or not, she was beginning to trust him on some level.

"I'd never do anything to jeopardize your career. I know how important it is for you to be seen as 'one of the guys.' Unless your safety was at stake, I'd never go behind your back. But just so you know, full disclosure and all that, if he'd tried to pair you with Jeff, I would've said something. There's no way I'd have you suffer two days with him."

He waited for the explosion. He was amazed when his words seemed to have the opposite effect on her.

Kina tried to bring herself under control. She knew Jonathan wouldn't go behind her back and ask to be paired with her just to get her in bed. She'd just automatically been a bitch to him. She didn't know how she knew he wouldn't try to set her up that way, but she knew it. He'd had plenty of times to make a move and he still hadn't even *kissed* her. She tried not to be upset about that. She knew Jonathan expected her to be upset with him for saying what he had about Jeff, but the truth was that she would've gone to Eddie herself and asked to be reassigned if he'd put Jeff with her. So she couldn't get mad that Jonathan would've done the same thing.

She brought her hand to her forehead and closed her eyes. "Crap. I'm sorry. That was bitchy of me to think, let alone say. I know you wouldn't have done that. I wasn't thinking."

Jonathan put his hand under her chin and watched as she opened her eyes and looked into his. "It's okay, hon. I don't know half the things you've probably gone through in your career to get where you are. I know most men in this industry are sexist. Just know I've got your back. And thanks for not being mad about the Jeff thing."

"I would've done the same thing," Kina told him honestly, echoing what she'd thought a moment ago. "I don't want to be alone with Jeff, forget being side-by-side with him, for three days in the wilderness."

Jonathan dropped his hand and they both laughed; glad the tension had been eased between them.

"I do have a question, though," Jonathan asked,

unable to hold it back. "Would you rather be stranded in Alaska in the cold or Africa in the heat?"

Kina laughed.

* * *

Kina and Jonathan watched as Roger and Darius tried to figure out what to do first, to set up their camp. Kina was watching Roger through her lens and Jonathan had Darius. She supposed the men weren't doing too badly, but it was obvious it was going to be a long two and a half days for them. Darius' profession as a chemist and Roger's vocation as a teacher weren't going to help them much in the Alaskan forest.

They knew enough to try to set up their sleeping quarters first. Kina didn't know much about wilderness camping either, as she wasn't really a camping kind of girl, but she didn't think the flimsy shelter they'd constructed would do them much good when it got dark and cold. But her role was to observe, so observe was what she was doing.

Kina and Jonathan continued to watch and film off and on while the guys tried to start putting together their raft. Their idea was to gather as many big logs as they could and attach them all together with the rope that Eddie had allowed each pair to have in their packs. On the surface it seemed like a good idea, but Kina wondered if they knew anything about what knots they should use, or how to lash the logs together, or even how many they should use. She mentally shrugged. It wasn't as if she knew those things either.

Jonathan put down his camera and leaned his elbows on his upraised knees. They'd sat down a while back because it was hard work to stand all day filming.

They'd used one of their emergency blankets for a barrier between the hard ground and their backsides. He looked at Kina sitting next to him, until she too put down her camera. He smiled at her.

"Think they have a chance at winning?"

"No way in hell," Kina answered, laughing quietly.

"Would you rather be stuck on a deserted island with four people you hate, or by yourself?"

"Easy, definitely by myself." Kina told him. Jonathan agreed.

Kina tried to think of a really good question. "Would you rather have the hiccups for the rest of your life or feel like you need to sneeze, but not be able to, for the rest of your life?"

Jonathan laughed so hard Roger and Darius looked over at them. Jonathan waved at them in apology before answering. "Oh my God, both of those options are so horrible. But I'd have to say the sneeze thing because I hate it when I have the hiccups. I can't imagine having them nonstop forever."

Kina just smiled. She couldn't believe she was sitting here, in the middle of Alaska, on the job, enjoying the hell out of being with a man. She stared at Jonathan's lips, wondering what they'd feel like on hers.

"You'd better stop looking at me like that, Kina, or I won't be responsible for my actions," Jonathan warned her seriously.

"How am I looking at you?"

"Like you want to have your wicked way with me."

Kina turned back toward the men struggling to tie two logs together, still grinning.

Jonathan shifted. He was hard and he hadn't even kissed her yet. The look she'd given him had made him want to throw her over his shoulder and head off to their tent for the rest of the night. She was sexy as hell and he wanted nothing more than to spend hours worshiping her. He sighed. It wasn't the time or the place, dammit. But if he had his way, he'd taste her lips before the night was up.

Later, as the sun was setting and after they'd eaten their pre-packaged meal, Kina watched uncomfortably as Darius tried unsuccessfully over and over, to light a fire. The men had gathered small sticks and some moss and had been trying to use the flint, with no luck. How anyone could fail at building a fire when they had a perfectly good flint was beyond her. She couldn't stand it anymore. The men were miserable. She looked around, as if someone would be standing in the woods spying on them, and leaned over to whisper to Jonathan.

"Do you think I should bring them a couple of matches? I mean, they look awful. I know Eddie doesn't want us helping them, but I hate just sitting here watching this."

Jonathan grinned at her. For all her brashness, she really was a softie. He whispered back, "I won't tell if you won't."

Kina smiled at him and walked toward Darius and Roger. She came back soon after, still grinning.

"Did they take them?" Jonathan asked, wondering if the men would try to play the game honestly or if they were too miserable to care anymore.

"They took them." Kina said simply. There was Jonathan's answer.

They watched as the fire the men were desperately trying to light suddenly came to life. The glow of the flames made its way across the distance to where Jonathan and Kina were sitting. There was no official rule that they couldn't go and sit with the men, but there *was* an unwritten one. Kina didn't really want to go and sit by the fire anyway, she was enjoying being with Jonathan in their own little dark world.

As darkness fell and the temperature got colder Jonathan put his arm around Kina and pulled her into his side. He argued with himself on whether or not he should make the play, but in the end decided to go for it.

God, he loved this woman. He hadn't admitted that to himself before, but he knew it was true. She was hardworking, honest, and a softie deep, down inside. Thinking about what she'd said about her last boyfriend, he couldn't stand the fact that someone had tried to crush her spirit. There was no way he'd want to tell her what to do all the time. He knew he'd have to try to curb his natural tendency to protect her, but he wasn't as bad as his brother was with that. Dean was the true alpha in their family. He decided to try to keep things light between them for the moment.

"Would you rather be illiterate, but able to read minds, or just have the ability to read?"

Kina had to think about that one for a moment. At first it seemed like a hard question, but the more she thought about it the easier it got.

"Definitely just have the ability to read. Think about it, after a while you'd be so sick of hearing what others thought. 'Should I order the nuggets or the burger?' 'Look at how fat he is.' 'I have to poop.'" She shuddered, but teased as she continued, "But I'd love to know what you're thinking half the time when you're looking at me."

Jonathan looked at the woman snuggled into his side and told her honestly, "I'll tell you what I'm thinking. I'm thinking how beautiful you are. I'm thinking how much I enjoy being around you and laughing with you. I'm thinking how badly I want to sink my hands in your hair and taste your lips. I'm wondering if you'll taste half as good as I've imagined."

Kina's breath caught. Holy Mother of God, he was good. Goosebumps broke out all down her arms. He was never afraid to put himself out there, emotionally. Did she dare do the same?

"I've wondered the same thing." She dared.

Jonathan immediately stood up and called over to the other men without responding to Kina's words. "We're hitting the sack. If you need anything, emergency-wise, just let us know. Otherwise, we'll see you in the morning."

The guys nodded and turned back to their fire, huddling as close as they dared to try to keep warm and ignoring the two camera crew.

Jonathan held his hand down to Kina. "Ready for bed?"

Chapter 7

Wow. Jonathan was looking at her in that intense way he had. Kina reached up to take hold of his hand. She had no idea what he had in mind, but for now, in this place, she trusted him. Was he going to escort her to her tent? Had what she said turned him off? Maybe this being honest thing wasn't working out after all.

Jonathan pulled Kina upright and headed to the two small tents they'd put up earlier. They'd set them up so they were facing each other and the doors opened toward each other. Jonathan walked around to the back of the tents, away from the other men and their fire. He never let go of Kina's hand. He stopped in front of the openings to the tents and turned Kina to face him. She really was tiny compared to him. He lifted her chin with one finger so she was looking into his eyes.

"There's nothing more I'd like to do than to take you inside one of our tents and make love to you all night long. I want to see your muscular little body more than I want my next breath. Unfortunately..." he blew out a long breath of air. They both watched as the chilly air turned it into a visible vapor. "It's way too cold, to do what I want to do. To take the time, to do what I want to do."

Kina's breath was coming in pants. She couldn't hide what she was feeling because of the coldness of the air. Every little puff that came from her mouth was being broadcasted to Jonathan, loud and clear. Whoa. She guessed her being honest worked after all. She wanted the same thing. The images his words brought to her mind were hot as hell. She could almost imagine him braced over her, his hair hanging down and brushing over her chest. She shuddered. How could she want this so quickly? She thought about it. Did she just want sex or was it Jonathan? She decided it was definitely Jonathan. No one else had made her feel this way in a long time.

Jonathan ran a finger down Kina's cheek and continued. "Even though it's too cold to make love to you tonight, I want you next to me. I want to feel you along my body. I want to hold you all night. I need to feel every inch of you curled up next to me. I'll understand if you think it's too soon. I won't force you, Kina, it's up to you. Just know I want this. I want this more than anything."

He stopped and actually took a small shuffling step away from her. He dropped his hands to his side. Kina was floored. He'd laid out what he'd wanted and was honest-to-God putting the decision in her hands. Matt would've just grabbed her and shoved her into the small tent.

She nodded at Jonathan. He took a step that brought him back in direct contact with her again. She could feel the heat from his body all along the front side of hers. He wasn't touching her, but if she took a deep breath she knew her breasts would brush against his chest. She craned her neck to look up at him.

"Say the words, hon."

Kina loved, and hated, that he wanted to hear her say what she wanted and he wouldn't just take a small nod from her as agreement.

"I'd love to spend the night curled up next to you," she told him simply and honestly. She had no idea where this was going, but for now she'd take it. It'd been so long since she'd cuddled with a man. She missed it. Matt hadn't been a cuddler. Once he'd gotten off, he turned over, with his back to her and went to sleep. She shook her head. She had to stop comparing everything Jonathan did to Matt. It wasn't fair to Jonathan or her. But then again, every time she *did* compare them, Jonathan always came out on top, so maybe it wasn't such a horrible thing after all.

Jonathan took her hand in his again and stepped toward his tent. He unzipped the opening and motioned for Kina to precede him into the small space. And it was small. These tents were made to hold one person. It'd be a tight fit, but Kina supposed that was what Jonathan envisioned.

Kina entered the tent, sat down, pulled off her boots and put them by the door. She scooted away from the opening and lay down on her side to give Jonathan room to enter. She watched as he first unzipped the other tent and grabbed the sleeping bag. He tossed it into his tent and then he also sat and removed his boots before scooting back and zipping up the flimsy door.

Kina was nervous. She wasn't sure what to do. She should've known Jonathan would take control. He pulled off his outer jacket and placed it where their heads would be. He turned to Kina and reached for the zipper of her jacket as well. Kina watched as he unzipped her jacket. She sat up to help him remove the coat. After placing her jacket next to his, he lay down on his side and put his head in his hand and just stared at her.

"What are you looking at?" Kina said nervously,

wondering when he'd start…whatever it was he was going to do.

"I'm savoring this moment. You have no idea how often I've dreamed about you in my bed." He chuckled. "Although this isn't really what I had in mind, but I'll take what I can get."

Kina didn't know what to say to that. He was so different from any man she'd ever met before in her life and she was so out of her element.

"Do you know how beautiful you are?" Jonathan asked quietly, still not moving to touch her in any way.

"I'm not beautiful." Kina told him honestly.

"You are," he insisted, finally moving. He took his index finger and ran it lightly over her eyebrows. Then he ran his finger down her nose and lightly traced her lips. Next, his finger roamed over her cheek to her ear. He continued tracing the contours of her face.

"Your skin is so soft. I've never felt anything like it. Your nose is small and slightly turned up at the end. Your lips are full and every time you speak I imagine what they'd taste like. You have cute little ears and your hair is your crowning glory. Oh, you're beautiful all right, Kina. So beautiful I have no idea how you haven't been snatched up by anyone else yet. But you haven't, and if I have anything to say about it, you won't be." He paused, looked away for a moment and then looked back into her eyes.

"What I'm about to say is probably going to freak you out, but I'm going to say it anyway. You're mine. *Mine*. I don't care how long it takes for you to realize it and understand that I'm not going anywhere. That I'll do whatever it takes to protect you from anyone who wants to hurt you. I'm not going to cheat on you; I'm not going to look elsewhere if you can't decide right away. I'll be here, waiting for you."

"Are you for real?" Kina couldn't believe what he was saying.

"I'm for real. This is real."

Kina closed her eyes. She was so confused. How could she even for a second *want* to hear that kind of thing from him? This wasn't the kind of woman she was. She couldn't deny his words made her feel good. More than good. They made her feel as if she finally had someone to count on. Who would be there for her? But at the same time, he was right, his words did freak her out. She wasn't sure what she was supposed to do with them. Her heart was beating what seemed to be a million miles an hour, she was scared, but his words also touched a place deep down inside of her. A part of her that wanted to be taken care of. That wanted to be wanted. She was confused and scared, but strangely, also felt safe. Here. With Jonathan. He wouldn't hurt her. He wouldn't rush her.

When she didn't say anything in response, Jonathan simply said, "Come here, it's cold and we need to get some sleep. Tomorrow will be a long day."

He turned over on his back and held his arm up so Kina could snuggle down against him. When she tentatively dropped down next to him he grasped one of her arms and pulled it over his chest. Her head was resting on his shoulder and she could feel his arm go around her back. He reached over and pulled the extra sleeping bag over the both of them.

She felt his arm rubbing sensuously over her back. Up and down. Up and down. God, it felt good. She was warm, comfortable lying against his chest and content. She never wanted the morning to come.

"Would you rather gain fifty pounds or lose fifty

pounds?"

Kina giggled. She loved this. She was so relaxed. It wasn't weird. It wasn't creepy. It was awesome. He totally got that she didn't want know what to say to his intimate words. He didn't push. He didn't insist she talk to him. He'd just changed the subject back to something light. They played the game for a while until she was so tired she couldn't stay awake anymore.

"This is nice," she said sleepily, losing the battle to stay awake. She was so comfortable.

"This *is* nice." Jonathan whispered back. "Sleep, hon. I'll be right here."

Kina smiled and fell asleep immediately.

* * *

Kina slowly came aware of her surroundings. It was still mostly dark outside and she couldn't understand what had woken her.

"No! Becky? Where are you? No!"

Kina remembered suddenly remembered where she was and who she was with. She could feel Jonathan thrashing in the throes of a nightmare beside her.

"Becky?" he yelled louder, obviously distraught.

Kina put her hand on his chest. "It's okay, wake up, Jonathan." She spoke firmly, trying to break the grip the dream had on him.

"I'm sorry, I'm so sorry." Jonathan sobbed, still stuck in whatever he was seeing in his dream world.

"Jonathan," Kina said more firmly. "Wake up."

After saying his name a few more times Kina saw his eyes open in the dim morning light and the bleakness she saw there made her gasp.

Jonathan shut his eyes tightly. Crap. He'd had the

damn dream again. He'd hoped he'd put it behind him, but it was obvious he hadn't.

"Talk to me," Kina said quietly, rubbing her hand over his chest soothingly.

Jonathan wanted nothing more than to get up and pace, to get away from the sympathy he could see in her eyes in the minimal light in the tent. Could he let her in? Was it too soon? Would she think badly of him? He knew he had to tell her, he'd just hoped it would be later.

Without opening his eyes, he put his hand over his face and scrubbed. "I'm not sure this is the right time to tell you," he told Kina honestly.

"If not now, when?" she asked stubbornly. She put her hand over his, resting on his face. "You said I was yours, I think I want that as well, but you have to talk to me. You have to let me in."

Crap. She was right. He knew she was right, but this was the hardest thing he'd ever had to do in his life. He hoped like hell she wouldn't look at him differently when he was done. His entire life felt like it was at stake. If she rejected him he didn't know what he'd do.

"You know what happened to Becky, my brother's wife, right?"

Kina simply said, "Yes, you know I do."

"I could have prevented it," Jonathan said bleakly, laying it right out there.

"Jonathan, you told me that before. I didn't believe it then and I don't believe it now."

He interrupted her before she could say anything else. He had to get this out all in one shot or he'd never be able to get through it.

"It's true. I went to the hotel that night. I knew something was wrong. I don't know how I knew it, I just did. I was worried about her. When the front desk clerk wouldn't tell me what room she was in, I let it go. He'd only connect me to her room via the phone and she didn't answer. I just left. I should've insisted. I should've called the police or something. I should've done more to find her. I left her there, for those men to hurt her." Jonathan said in anguish. "I left her there," he said again, in a whisper.

Kina came up on an elbow and leaned over Jonathan, getting in his face so he couldn't ignore her words. "It wasn't your fault, Jonathan."

When he didn't say anything she knew she wasn't getting to him. She tried a different tactic. "What did Becky say? Does she blame you?" When he didn't answer she continued. "What about your brother? Does he blame you for what happened to his woman? Did he tell you it was your fault?"

"No," Jonathan said softly.

"Why don't you believe them? Do you really think they'd lie to you? Do you really think Becky would be doing so well if they blamed you? If she still held some angst toward you?" She tried one last question to try to get through to him. "Would your brother still want you to come home and work with him if he thought you were in *any* way responsible for what happened to Becky?"

Jonathan didn't say anything. Kina leaned down and brushed her lips over his cheek, then his forehead, then finally his lips. She kept her mouth close to his and said resolutely, her lips brushing his with each word. "It. Is. Not. Your. Fault."

Jonathan didn't say anything, but his arms came up around her, knocking her off balance. She fell onto his chest and his lips claimed hers. He left her no room to back off, no room to say no. He conquered her mouth with his. His tongue swept inside her mouth, curling around hers and memorizing her taste, the feel of her. He ran his tongue over her teeth, around and over her tongue, and finally he drew back, nipping her lips with his teeth before curling his hand around the back of her neck and bringing her forehead to rest against his. He didn't apologize for the rough kiss he'd stolen. Her hair fell around them, cocooning them into their own private world.

He'd needed her more than anything he could remember ever needing before in his life. She was his. He wasn't going to let her go. He couldn't bring himself to apologize for the kiss, even if she hadn't wanted it or initiated it. He'd *needed* it.

"I dream I'm looking for her everywhere, but I can't find her. I'm calling her name over and over and I know she's there, but she's not answering me. I'm in a hallway and trying to open all the doors. I know she's behind one of them, but I don't know which one. All the doors are locked and I'm just going up and down the hall trying to get into the rooms yelling for her. Finally I get to a room and the door is unlocked. I open it and she's lying on the floor. Bloody and beaten. She opens her eyes and looks up at me. She says 'Why didn't you find me earlier?' She blames me in my dream. It's always the same. I never find her in time and she wants to know why."

Kina tried to concentrate. Holy hell, that kiss had knocked her socks off. It was so hot. He hadn't asked if it was okay, he hadn't let her take the lead, he'd stolen the kiss, and she'd loved every second of it. He took it from her and she'd gladly let him. This man was hurting and needed her. *Her*. No one had ever needed her that badly before.

"You have to stop torturing yourself," she

whispered. "Becky and Dean wouldn't want this for you. You said it yourself, she's doing great. Yes, what she went through sucked, but she's happy now. No one blames you, but yourself. You have to forgive yourself, Jonathan. Look at it this way. If the same thing happened today, would you do everything the same as you did then?" She didn't even have to wait for him to answer. "No, you wouldn't. Learn from what happened and move on. For your sake, for their sake," her voice lowered even more, "for our sake, move on."

Jonathan's eyes opened and peered into her own. They were face to face. She saw the guilt burning in his eyes, but she also thought she saw hope. "I'll try, Kina. I'll try, but if I slip, I hope you'll be there to help me up."

Kina nodded. "I will, Jonathan. I will."

It was enough, for now.

"I'm sorry about the kiss, hon."

Kina smiled. This she could deal with. "I'm not."

"You're not?"

"How could I be? That was the hottest good morning kiss I've ever received. Hell, it was the hottest kiss I've ever received." Kina loved to see the smile come over his face. Man he was hot, and for now, he was hers. She couldn't help but tease him, glad they were getting back to their lighthearted banter. "But you *did* say I could be in charge, remember?"

Jonathan smirked. He brought his hands up away from her body and clasped them together under his head in a relaxed pose. "By all means, take charge." He challenged her, hoping like hell she'd take him up on it.

Kina looked down at the broad chest she'd been lying on. The sun had finally started making its way over the horizon and allowed just enough light to admire him with. His long hair was spread out over their makeshift pillow and the sweatshirt he was wearing was stretched tight over his abs and chest. She licked her lips. This was going to be fun.

"You'll keep your arms there?" She asked innocently running one finger down the center of his chest toward his waistband. She swore she heard him growl.

"Careful hon, you might bite off more than you can chew."

Kina laughed. "Oh, I think I can handle what you've got." She bent down and nipped his chin. Yup, that was definitely a growl, but she was impressed with his control as he kept his hands clenched together under his head.

"Kiss me. God, please kiss me." He bit out.

Kina couldn't tease him anymore. She wanted him as much as he apparently wanted her. She leaned down and licked his bottom lip. Before he could do anything else she grabbed his lip with her teeth and pulled. That was it. His control was gone.

He sat up, grabbed her by the shoulders and spun her around in the small space. Kina found herself on her back with Jonathan leaning over her. He slammed his lips down on hers once again and they battled for control. Kina wasn't going to passively lie there and let Jonathan do whatever he wanted. She let her hands wander while their tongues dueled and their teeth nipped and pulled at each other. She worked her way under the back of his sweatshirt and under his T-shirt and let her nails lightly scrape their way up his back as far as she could get them to go. She whimpered when he drew back from her mouth to stare down at her.

He didn't say a word, but he flattened his hand and

drew it down over her chest, over her breastbone, over her bellybutton to the button on her jeans. He didn't unbutton it, but worked her own T-shirt out of her pants and moved his hand underneath. God almighty. His hand was chilly from the morning air and she could feel the calluses covering the palm of his hand. He worked his way upward, never losing eye contact with her, until he reached her belly button. One finger swirled around it and lightly pressed in.

She couldn't help it, the question just popped into her head and she couldn't hold it back. "Would you rather have an innie or an outie?" She watched as Jonathan didn't say anything, but smiled and dropped his lips back to hers.

As they kissed and continue to learn the contours of each other's mouth, his hand moved upward again. He went as far up as the bottom of her bra then stopped, running his fingers over the bottom underwire sensuously. Over and over, his fingers caressed the skin just under her bra. Goosebumps rose all over her skin and she could feel his grin as he felt them too. Her nipples were hard and she swore she could feel them ache.

Jonathan's long hair was hanging around them and Kina imaged how it would feel to have his hair brushing over her bare chest, as he suckled at her breasts. Her breath came out in short choppy pants.

Kina dug her nails into Jonathan's lower back a bit harder, not hard enough to break his skin, but enough to let him know she was loving what he was doing to her body and what she *wanted* him to do to her body.

Just as Jonathan's hands started to skim over the cups of her bra they heard, "Good morning!" ring out from across the clearing. Damn.

Jonathan raised his head from hers and they both stilled. Kina couldn't help but giggle. Jonathan shook his head and smiled down at Kina. "I did say last night, this wasn't what I wanted to happen, but I can't be sorry. You feel so good, hon. I can't wait to get you alone."

Kina slowly removed her hands from Jonathan's skin soothing his skin where she'd dug her nails in and brought one hand up to his scruffy face. "I can't wait either."

Jonathan reluctantly slid his hands back down her belly and smoothed her T-shirt back down. He cupped her cheeks in his and leaned down to give her a sweet kiss on the lips. "As much as I want to feel your heat surrounding me, we'll take our time. You deserve to be wooed."

"Wooed? Who says that?"

"I do," answered Jonathan with a smile. "Now, how about we get this show on the road? Eddie would have our heads if we didn't get the guys' morning routine on film."

Kina nodded. As much as she wanted to stay in this little tent with Jonathan all day, they had a job to do.

To give the men credit, they didn't say anything when Kina and Jonathan got out of the same tent that morning. Kina figured they were just too miserable to care what the camera operators were doing. Their shelter had held up through the night, but it wasn't very much protection from the biting wind and the cold weather. They'd managed to keep the fire going throughout the night and it was blazing when Kina had finished brushing her teeth and using the little girls' 'tree.'

Kina had never liked keeping her distance from the contestants. It just seemed cold to watch people day in and day out and not talk to them. She'd tried to refrain from getting to know Sam, from the Australia show, but that didn't last very long, especially after Sam had saved her life. The two of them had forged a close friendship that she treasured today. Kina hated what Eddie had done to her and Alex and was so glad they'd managed to end up together despite the underhanded tricks Eddie played on them both on the set and during the editing process.

While Kina knew she'd never be close to Darius and Roger like she was with Sam, she still made the effort. She wandered over to their fire and held her hands out. Even though she'd been snuggled up to Jonathan all night, the air this morning was chilly and the flames felt good on her fingers.

"What's up for the day, gentlemen?" she asked politely.

"Trying to get that damn raft to float," Roger answered for them both. "We've tried everything we can to get the darn thing to stay together when we put it on the lake, but the knots we've tied always come undone. Got any advice for us?" he asked hopefully.

Jonathan piped in before Kina could say anything. "Sorry guys, that one's outside our expertise."

Kina looked over at him. She hadn't heard him come up behind her. She wasn't sure if he'd answered because he thought she'd jump in to help the men or what. She relaxed when she saw him wink at her. Okay, then.

The day actually went by pretty quickly after they ate breakfast. Darius and Roger headed down to the lake and Kina and Jonathan spent the better part of the morning filming their trials, and sometimes heated discussions, on how to get the raft to be seaworthy.

They took a break for lunch, a few hours later. Jonathan and Kina wandered a bit away from the men to eat, simply because they didn't want to flaunt the fact that they had a nice well-rounded lunch, and the men only had the remains of their one MRE.

Jonathan found a flat rock in the sun and gestured for Kina to sit. He brought over their supplies and pulled out two oranges, bread, sliced turkey, slightly wilted lettuce, and two small bags of potato chips.

Kina peeled the oranges while Jonathan put together their sandwiches. Kina thought for what seemed the hundredth time, how well the two of them worked together. She hated to keep comparing Jonathan to Matt, but she couldn't help it. Matt would've made her do everything while he glared at her in displeasure.

There were so many differences between the two men it wasn't even fair to compare them. Jonathan had opened up to her that morning. He'd made himself vulnerable to her and shown her a side of himself, she knew many people didn't get to see. He felt deeply. He wasn't the kind of man to let things go easily. On the surface he came across as a typical macho man who wanted to be in charge, but by his actions, over and over, he'd proven to her to have hidden depths.

Jonathan held out a sandwich to her. They sat and ate in companionable silence. The sandwiches tasted awesome. Kina wasn't sure if it was because of where they were, but she knew she'd remember this little picnic for the rest of her life. Nothing with Jonathan was as she'd experienced before. So far she'd loved every second of her time spent with him. He was courteous and attentive, but not suffocating. He was also fun to be around.

"Would you rather have to eat nothing other than fruits or vegetables for the rest of your life, or only able to eat meat?"

Jonathan laughed. He loved the scenarios Kina could come up with. They always seemed appropriate to their circumstances. He noticed they'd both finished eating their sandwiches and were eating their oranges. He got a wicked idea.

Kina startled when Jonathan reached over and took her hand in his. He lifted it up to his mouth and put her index finger in his mouth and sucked the juice off. She could feel his tongue swirl around her knuckle sensuously. Gah. Two could play at that game.

She grabbed his hand that was holding hers and returned the gesture, only hers was much more suggestive of what she'd like to do to him later. She twirled her tongue around his finger and took the entire thing into her mouth down to the knuckle, then sucked hard. She watched, fascinated as his cheeks flushed, and his eyes dropped into slits. She probably shouldn't poke the bear, but it was so much fun.

Jonathan tried to get himself under control. My God, this woman was dangerous. She was lucky he was a gentleman and wanted to take his time the first time he had her.

"I've never been with someone like you."

Jonathan turned toward Kina and lifted his eyebrows. He'd wanted her to open up to him, but it wasn't something that could be rushed. Kina had to do it on her own and at her own pace. He was floored when she not only opened herself up, but laid herself bare. He grasped her hand, offering silent support, while she continued talking.

"When I was growing up, I never knew my dad. My mom worked really hard to keep a roof over our heads and keep food on the table. She was a good parent, but just not there much for me, emotionally. We moved around a lot, she was always trying to find a better job and more money, but unfortunately, that always seemed out of reach. When I was sixteen, she had a heart attack and died."

"Where was your dad?"

"He wasn't around. Mom never talked about him much, only to tell me that once he heard she was pregnant, he left. He didn't want a kid and as far as I know he never even saw me."

Jonathan heard the pain in her voice. "That's his loss, Kina."

She nodded, then continued. "I moved in with a

friend of mine from school until I graduated. I had one boyfriend in high school. I thought we were good. I'd been planning on trying to get into the same college he was going to attend. One day, I heard through the grapevine at school, he'd been cheating on me. When I asked him about it he just shrugged and told me what we had was never serious. It was only a fling and he couldn't believe I'd thought we were going to stay together. It hurt."

Jonathan's arm wrapped around her shoulders and pulled her into his side. Kina couldn't get distracted now. She had to keep going. He'd opened up to her this morning, she could do the same. "Then I met Matt. He seemed to be everything I'd ever wanted. He wanted to take care of me and I wanted to be taken care of. My mom hadn't done that great of a job at it and my high school boyfriend hadn't wanted me either. At first it was great. He was paying all the bills; he drove me where I wanted to go. He did stuff I thought was courteous and helpful, like get my phone messages for me and answer my phone. After a while he got more and more 'helpful.' He wouldn't let me go anywhere without him. I soon lost touch with any friends I did have in high school. He made himself the center of my world."

"He'd get crazy jealous whenever we went anywhere. If the guy bagging our groceries smiled at me, he'd threaten him. God forbid when we went out, if someone talked to me. He'd lose it. When we'd get home, he'd accuse me of leading men on. The sex became more and more scary. He'd hold me down and put his hand over my mouth to keep me quiet as he took me. He didn't care about foreplay or making sure I wanted any of what he was doing to me."

"I knew it was out of control. I didn't know how I'd

gotten there. How did me wanting someone to take care of me, turn into that? Finally, one day when he'd gone to work, I wrote him a note, packed up what I could, and just left."

"Have you ever heard from him since, hon?"

"No, never. It was as if once I left, he forgot all about me. That's definitely a good thing." Kina paused, getting to the point of her story. "I can't go back to that, Jonathan. Matt taught me a lot about myself. I can't be owned. I might like having someone pay attention to me and do things for me, but being 'taken care of' isn't want I want anymore."

Jonathan turned Kina toward him. He looked in her eyes and hoped she could see his sincerity. "I don't want to control you, love. I can't deny I want to take care of you, but not like he did. I want to make sure you're comfortable. I want to be there for you when you've had a bad day. I want to make your lunch for you. I want to drive you places, but not to be controlling, but to just be with you for an extra five minutes of the day. When I say you're 'mine,' I don't mean as a possession. I mean you're mine to protect, to care for, to be with, to care about." He couldn't say 'love,' it was too soon. Oh, he meant that, but figured it was too soon for her to hear it.

"I'm not him. I'll do everything in my power to try to make that clear to you. I love that you can take charge. I love that you're independent. There's no way I want to decide what you should wear each day or even make all the decisions about what we should eat and when. I just don't want you ever to be too independent to want me around."

Kina took a deep breath. "Just give me time."

"You got it, hon. You got it."

Jonathan leaned toward her and kissed her gently

on the forehead. He then gathered up their trash and tried to get both of them back on an even keel. They still had a long day ahead of them and he knew they had to get going. After putting their lunch things away he looked down at Kina, pulled her hand up to his mouth and kissed it tenderly.

"Ready to go?"

At her nod he dropped her hand and they both grabbed up their cameras and headed back towards the contestants.

The rest of the afternoon was much the same as the morning. Roger and Darius had finally seemed to get the hang of the knots and lashings they needed to make their raft float. It was a good thing they'd only have one more night outside, however, because their tempers were flaring and it was clear they were ready to have a break from one another.

That night, the four of them sat around the fire for a while, talking about their lives back home and why the two contestants decided they wanted to be on a reality show. Kina wasn't surprised to hear they'd thought they'd be on a different kind of show.

"I agreed to be on the show because I thought it was a bachelorette type of show," Roger said. "It was only right before we were to leave to come up here Eddie told us the show had changed."

Darius agreed. "Yeah, I'm not really cut out for this type of thing. But I figured I'd already told everyone I was going to be on television, so I might as well still come."

"But he did give you a chance to back out?" Kina asked curiously.

"Yes, from what I understand, there were a few guys who refused to come, after hearing it was some sort of 'ultra man' challenge thing." Roger answered.

Kina nodded. She'd thought it was odd there were only twelve men to start with. That number seemed low. But Eddie obviously hadn't wanted to open auditions again so he went with what he had.

"So far," Darius went on, "the show's been kinda lame. The challenges haven't been too hard, especially since they're trying to make this show out to be some sort of macho man thing. But I suppose that's okay with us since we weren't really prepared for it."

Kina had to agree. After the sun started to set, Kina looked over at Jonathan. Would he want to sleep in the same tent tonight? She was so nervous. She wanted to sleep with him again, but only sleep. She wasn't ready for more…yet. She felt pretty raw after sharing her relationship with Matt, with him. She didn't think Jonathan was the type of man to run scared after hearing something like that, but how well did she really know him after all?

Jonathan was waiting for Kina to look at him. He'd been ready to hit the sack a while back, but was enjoying the camaraderie Kina had with the two men. She was fascinating to watch. Her natural, bubbly personality made people want to confide in her. He gestured with his head towards their tents, asking nonverbally if she was ready. She nodded and picked herself up off the ground.

"We're going to head off to sleep," she said half-apologetically, knowing she'd be warm and relatively comfortable tonight, while they'd have to sleep on the hard ground and in the cold again.

Jonathan was feeling pretty mellow until Roger opened his mouth.

"Yeah, wish I could have me some of that," he said

not too quietly.

Jonathan was in his face before anyone could react. “You want to say that again?”

“Ah, no, sorry,” Roger stammered, obviously taken aback at how quickly Jonathan had gone from friendly cameraman to pissed-off in-his-face male.

Jonathan glared at him some more and said before turning back toward Kina, “No one disrespects my woman. *Espccially* not in front of mc…got it?”

He watched as Roger nodded furiously and dropped his eyes to the ground and away from him.

Satisfied, he reluctantly turned back toward Kina. He had no idea how she’d react to his actions. After all she’d told him, he figured she’d probably be pissed. She’d told him often enough how she hated to be treated like she couldn’t take care of herself. But when he’d heard the crude words coming from Roger he just reacted. He couldn’t have sat there and allowed him to diss Kina like that. No way.

When Jonathan turned around he saw Kina standing with her arms folded across her chest…grinning.

Thank God.

He didn’t say anything, but put his arm around her and rested his hand at the small of her back before steering them toward their tents. He waited to hear what she had to say. It didn’t take long; they hadn’t even made it ten steps when she said, “God, that was hot.”

He smiled.

“Would you rather have a guy fight for you or over you?”

He wasn’t expecting an answer, but heard her say under her breath, “For me.”

* * *

As Jonathan lay in his tent with Kina in his arms, he thought about what would happen after the show was over. He knew he was headed back to Arizona for good. He was telling Kina the truth when he'd explained that he wasn't cut out to be a camera operator anymore. He was excited about his new career. He didn't know what Kina thought was happening between them, though. Sure, he'd told her she was his, but he didn't know if she really understood what that meant or what he'd meant by it.

They'd had a lot of serious talks lately, but he figured he might as well start one more. He hated to disturb the sweet feeling of her lying in his arms. She fit him perfectly and he could imagine them falling asleep this way every night for the rest of their lives, but that was the problem. He had no idea if she also could see that, or even if she wanted it.

"You awake?" he asked Kina softly.

"Yeah," she murmured sleepily.

"What are your plans for after this show is over?" he asked bluntly, not beating around the bush. He might as well throw it out there. He knew Kina would rather he be upfront and honest than prevaricate.

Kina was tired and half-asleep, until she heard the seriousness behind Jonathan's question. She had no idea how to answer him. She knew what she wanted, but she wasn't sure what he wanted to hear.

She decided to tread carefully. "Eddie's offered to sign me on for another three show contract, but I'm not sure I want to keep working for him. I'm not thrilled with the way he treats people and what he's done to the contestants on his shows in the past."

She squirmed when Jonathan didn't answer right away.

"What if I asked you to come back to Arizona with me?" he finally asked.

God. Kina didn't know how to answer him. It was way too soon for her to be thinking about moving to a different state for a man…wasn't it?

"I don't know what to say," she told him honestly. And she didn't. She wanted to jump up and scream 'Yes!' but the more practical side of her said she didn't even know this man.

"Say yes," Jonathan urged, but said no more.

"What would I do there?"

Jonathan wanted to tell her that she didn't have to do anything but love him, but he knew that'd sound crazy. And besides, Kina was the type of woman who needed to do something; she needed to feel like she was contributing. She'd never let him earn all the money.

"I don't know," he said honestly, "but I'd help you find whatever it was that you wanted to do there. All I know is I want you with me. I don't want to leave in a few weeks and never see you again. You're all I've ever wanted in my life. More than I ever thought I'd have. I want to introduce you to my folks as mine, have you see how happy they are on the animal refuge they run. I know you saw them when you were there for the last show, but I want you to *know* them. I want to have double dates with my brother and Becky."

"You're so smart, Kina; if you want to stay in television, I'm sure you'll find your way to do that. We have lots of TV stations there, with your experience, someone will snatch you up quickly. If you want to do something else, we'll figure that out too. I just want to share my life with you, however you'll let me."

Kina teared up. She was thankful it was dark in the tent and Jonathan couldn't see her. "I'll have to think about it," she finally said, once she had her emotions under control. "I've been at the mercy of a man before, I told you about that," she told him honestly. "I don't know if I can do it again." She felt him nod, but he kept silent.

"I'm not asking you to be at my mercy, hon. If anything, I'm at *your* mercy. You could tell me you wanted to live on a nudist colony and I'd be helpless to deny you anything. If you wanted to get your own place, I'd understand. I want you to feel comfortable and not feel like I'm smothering you. It would kill me to have you living there and not in my arms every night, but I understand why you'd need that. I do."

Quiet settled. They both had a lot to think about.

When Kina didn't think he'd say anything else before they fell back asleep, he surprised her.

"All my life I've heard from my dad about how he met my mom. He told me and Dean stories about how when we found the woman for us, we'd know immediately. We'd take one look and know she was the *One*. Kina, I swear I thought he was crazy. There was no way anyone could do that. It wasn't logical. Dean and I always laughed at him behind his back. Then Dean met Becky. He told me it was exactly as Dad had explained to us. He met her and knew she was it for him. He was done. Period. I still didn't really believe the whole thing. I mean, it's ridiculous...Then I met you."

Silence filled the tent again. *What was he saying? Was he saying...no.*

"Jonathan," Kina started. She had no idea what she was going to say, but Jonathan interrupted her by putting his fingers across her lips. His fingers were warm against her mouth. She felt his lips skim across the top of her head.

"Don't say anything, love. I know it's crazy and hard to believe, hell, I didn't believe it and I had the proof in my dad and ancestors right there in my face my entire life. But you're it for me. If you don't want to go to Arizona, I'll go wherever you want to go. I'll follow you around as you advance your career. I don't care. I'll stay at home and clean and cook and do your laundry. Whatever it takes. I won't lie, I was looking forward to working with Dean and living near my family, but you mean more to me than all of that. You think about it. Whatever you want to do, I'll be there, if you'll let me."

Kina didn't like it. Not at all. She didn't want to be his *One*. She wasn't good enough for him. How could he feel that for her? She had so many questions and so many doubts. It was too much pressure.

Jonathan sighed. He knew it was too soon for him to reveal his feelings, but he couldn't help it. He loved her. Period. He'd let her think about what he said and hope like hell he didn't just chase her away for good.

He put his hand on the back of her head and just held her to him. "Shhhh, don't say anything. Just go to sleep. No pressure, hon. I swear. Just sleep. We'll talk about it later."

He felt her nod. Neither fell asleep right away.

Kina woke up first in the morning. Jonathan had slept peacefully through the night and hadn't had any nightmares, at least none that had woken her up. She lay there waiting for the day to start, enjoying the feeling of being held tight. Even in his sleep, Jonathan hadn't loosened his hold on her. It felt…good. Not stifling, as it would have felt if another man held her like that. She breathed in the smell of him. He hadn't shaved in the time they'd been out there, and the beginnings of his dark beard were sexy as hell. She would've gotten up, but somehow knew if she moved, he'd immediately wake up. She was enjoying being close to him and listening to him lightly snore.

She thought about everything he'd told her last night. She had been way freaked out, but this morning, lying in his arms, she'd mellowed. She had no idea why, but she believed him. She'd seen Dean with Becky. She'd even seen his parents with each other. There was something about their relationships that seemed magical. She never saw any of them being overbearing or too controlling. Yes, Dean was pretty protective, but Becky never complained. The more Kina thought about it, the more the tight ball of doubt in her stomach was loosening.

Eventually, Jonathan began to stir. The real world would intrude on their idyllic time soon enough. She looked in his eyes as they opened for the first time.

"What time is it?" he mumbled sleepily.

"I have no idea." She decided to go on as if their emotional discussion the night before hadn't happened. There'd be time to re-hash it and figure everything out later. "Would you rather have to wake up at six am every morning no matter what, or not be able to go to sleep until one am?" As far as a question, it was kinda lame, but Jonathan laughed anyway. He squeezed her once and stretched.

"I'll go out first, give you some time to get changed, unless you want to go first?"

Kina nodded and waved him on. He was always looking out for her, never forcing her to do things his way. Would that annoy her down the line? Would it get old? She wasn't sure. She wasn't submissive, but it was nice to be taken care of now and then. She'd been honest with him about that. She figured it had a lot to do with her childhood, when she'd not really had anyone to take care of her. She sighed. She was worrying herself to death. She decided to just take the day as it came and not worry about anything other than getting the best shots for the show.

Darius and Roger were actually still sleeping by the time she and Jonathan had finished getting ready. Kina filmed some quick shots of them sleeping that could be spliced into the final version of the show, then helped Jonathan pack up their tents. They'd be picked up today and the competition would commence to see whose raft floated the best in the lake.

Not too much later, the two men woke up and started their morning. They didn't have any food left, having eaten it all the days before, and they hadn't found anything else to eat near the campsite. They were grumpy and tired, and it showed. Kina tried not to laugh. It wasn't nice, but she knew it'd make for great reality TV.

At noon on the dot, Eddie came striding into the camp area. Kina had no idea where he came from, but thought it was funny he'd just sort of appeared out of thin air. He asked Darius and Roger if they were ready to go and simply nodded when an emphatic 'yes' was the answer.

They all trudged down to where a boat was waiting on the lake. It had Benedict and Nash in it already, along with Taylor. The plan was to collect everyone and meet Shannel back at a rendezvous point. They'd film some of the ceremony there and then make the rounds to each of the campsites where the men would show off their rafts and attempt to make the six-hundred-yard round trip, to prove their raft was seaworthy. Of course on television, it would be seamless and the traveling from campsite to campsite wouldn't be shown. More of the magic of editing and television.

It was a pretty sad group that gathered with Shannel. Trent and Ian apparently weren't speaking with each other because of something that happened back at their campsite. Roger and Darius weren't too bad, although Roger looked like he had a three-week beard instead of just a three-day one. Benedict and Nash looked like they hadn't slept at all in the last three days.

Shannel went around the group, asking the men how they fared, whether they'd had anything to eat besides the one MRE they were given, and if they were able to light a fire with the flint they were given.

Kina was scared that Roger and Darius were going to spill the beans about how she'd cheated and given them a few matches, but she should've known better.

There was no way they were going to let anyone know what had happened. They were too thankful they'd had fire to give her away.

The others had also managed, from what they'd said, to light their fire. It seemed that was the best thing that happened to any of them, however. Trent and Ian fought over every aspect of their time out in the wilderness. Trent had wanted to build the raft one way and Ian disagreed. So they'd spent the first day and a half arguing about it. They didn't want to cooperate with each other in building a place to sleep because they were so mad at each other, so they suffered as a result of that as well. Since Ian was a restaurant owner, he had all sorts of ideas about how to find food, but Trent's occupation as a nurse made him wary of eating anything that wasn't packaged and 'pre-approved.' All in all, it sounded like they'd had a perfectly miserable time. Kina knew they would be highlighted pretty heavily in the airing of the show. While Eddie might not like drama personally, it made for great television.

Kina thought Roger and Darius' recounting of their time by the lake was actually pretty boring, especially compared to Ian and Trent's. She knew Eddie would cut most of it from the show. There just wasn't anything fun to watch about two people getting along and not having anything dramatic happen.

Benedict and Nash had a close call with a bear while they were sleeping one night. Apparently Nash hadn't put away the trash from their MRE very well and they'd heard a bear around their site. They panicked and didn't know what to do, but Taylor had taken one of his camera lights and shone it at the bear. Luckily, the bright light scared it enough, that it ambled away. Of course Taylor hadn't gotten that part on film, much to

Eddie's chagrin, but he did manage to get some footage of the bear walking away into the woods surrounding the lake. It was a good shot, just enough drama to use as a teaser for the show.

The contestants were all loaded up into one boat with Shannel, Eddie, and Carl, and the rest of the crew climbed into another. They headed off to Trent and Ian's campsite and raft first.

Jeff couldn't control himself and just had to act like an ass, while they were headed away from the dock.

"So…you two have a good time out in the wilderness?"

Jonathan didn't answer, trying to control himself for Kina's sake, but glared at Jeff instead. Kina could've told him that wouldn't shut the other man up.

"Seriously, did you use body heat to keep warm? Wish I was paired up with you, baby, I would've found some creative ways to keep you warm a-l-l night long."

Before Kina could put a hand on Jonathan to keep him calm, he'd taken Jeff by the collar and was actually holding him over the side of the fast-moving boat. Crap!

"If you ever lay a hand on her, you'll regret it. Hear me?"

Kina quickly put her camera down and instead of pulling on Jonathan, she knew that wouldn't do any good, she leaned over Jonathan, putting her hand on the small of his back to steady herself and leaned over the side of the boat to put her face right up next to Jeff's.

"As if I'd let you anywhere near me Jeff. Stick with your groupie chicks, you'll never get any of this!"

Jonathan realized what he'd done the second he felt Kina's hand on his back. *Ah, crap.* Oh well, it was too late to take it back. It was the third time he'd acted without thinking when someone had spoken crap to

Kina. She'd forgiven him twice; he wasn't sure how long his luck would hold out if he kept it up. He was shocked to hear Kina's scowled words at Jeff. Although he supposed he shouldn't be. She could hold her own, he knew it, but there was no way he'd leave her to fight her own battles. She was his. He'd protect her no matter who or what was threatening her. And Jeff's words were definitely a threat.

He pulled back, bringing Jeff upright with him, and Jonathan could still feel Kina's hand on his back. She was lightly rubbing in little circles, as if to calm him down. And surprisingly, it was working. Just her touch alone could ground him.

As soon as he had his balance, Jeff shrugged off Jonathan's hold. "I was just kidding man, geez!"

They all knew he hadn't been joking, but in order to let it drop, they all backed off. Kina picked her camera off the floor and waited for them to arrive at the campsite. She wasn't sure why she wasn't more pissed. If it had been any other man, or even if this had happened before she and Jonathan had spent those two days and nights talking and sharing emotional experiences, she would've gone off. She was perfectly able to speak for herself and put Jeff in his place. But now, knowing Jonathan the way she did, she felt warm inside. It was obvious he was trying to tone down any he-man tendencies he might have, but to have someone so willing to stick up for her was a heady feeling. One she was very afraid she could get used to.

* * *

It was decided the camera operators for each pair of contestants would film their portion of the raft contest, so Kina and Jonathan could just watch from a distance as Benedict and Nash tried to paddle the six hundred yards on their raft. Kina thought they just might have a chance. Their raft seemed to be very sturdy and at first, they were doing great. They'd made it three hundred yards out and had started back towards the shore when it started tipping.

Nash tried to compensate for Benedict's weight sliding toward the water but couldn't quite recover the raft. It made for an excellently framed shot. Benedict fell into the water with a huge splash and the raft tipped all the way up. This, consequently, literally threw Nash from the tallest point on the raft, head-over-heels into the water. The raft flipped completely upside down. If the contest was being held in Florida this wouldn't have been a big deal, but because it was Alaska, in late September, it was a serious situation.

The water was not warm. Everyone standing around knew the men didn't have a lot of time, before they'd start freezing, literally. The motorized boat was there, ready to fish the contestants out of the water if needed, but first it was obvious they wanted to try to get back on their raft and finish the competition. After a few attempts, everyone standing on the bank watching knew it wasn't going to be possible. Every time Benedict tried to get back on, the raft tipped almost vertically so he couldn't manage it. They got smart and Nash tried to balance it out on the other side, but as soon as Benedict got halfway on and Nash tried to get on as well, it would tip.

After about five minutes of the men gallantly trying to board their craft, the medic on the boat called it quits. The two men were fished out of the lake and their sad little raft was towed back to shore.

Kina wasn't one to laugh at anyone's misfortune, but they had looked pretty funny. She was just glad it wasn't her in the cold water. While everyone else was warm and dry on the bank, Ian said just loud enough for those standing around to hear, "What doesn't kill you, makes you stronger."

Kina almost lost it when Jonathan leaned toward her and whispered for her ears only, "Except for bears, bears will kill you." It was especially funny since they were all currently standing in prime bear territory. It was funny, but not funny at the same time. Kina mock-glared at Jonathan and said primly, "Shhhh, behave!"

They shared a smile at the joke.

When the men got back to shore, everyone could see that the medic had provided them with emergency blankets to warm their core body temperature. The men were fine health-wise. Wet, cold, and upset they couldn't make it back to shore on the raft, but fine.

Everyone re-boarded the boats to make their way to Roger and Darius' camp so those two could try out their home-made raft. Apparently, making a raft from scratch was harder than it looked. Roger and Darius started out well, just as Benedict and Nash had, but they had issues even before they'd made it to the three hundred yard mark. There wasn't anything dramatic about the failure of their raft, they just suddenly started sinking. One minute they were there on the lake paddling hard, the next they were up to their waists in water, then everyone saw logs floating all around them and all that could be seen of them was their heads bobbing above the waterline.

They were quickly hauled into the safety boat as well. Benedict and Nash high-fived each other. Because they'd gone further than Roger and Darius, they would be staying on the show. It was up to Trent and Ian to beat the benchmark that had just been set by Roger and Darius.

Shortly after everyone arrived at their campsite, it was pretty obvious that Trent and Ian would be going home. Their raft looked like it had been built by a bunch of kids. There were large spaces between the logs they'd tried to lash together, which by itself wouldn't necessarily mean the raft wouldn't float, but the lashings were unevenly spaced and the knots didn't look right. Kina figured that if she, someone who knew nothing about what a knot on a homemade raft was supposed to look like, thought they looked weird, then the duo was doomed.

Kina was amazed the raft actually made it about forty yards offshore before suddenly coming apart. Much like Roger and Darius' raft, one moment Trent and Ian were sitting on the logs paddling and the next, there were logs floating all around them and the men were treading water. Unlike Roger and Darius, the two men immediately started yelling at each other and blaming the other for their failure.

Because they were so close to shore they weren't picked up by the emergency boat, but they simply swam back to where everyone was standing instead. The second they could stand, Ian threw a punch at Trent. Apparently, Trent saw it coming and ducked, but instead of taking the higher road and ignoring his partner, he swung right back at Ian. The fight was definitely on.

Kina didn't bother picking up her camera to film; she figured Jeff and Carl had it under control. She noticed that Jonathan subtly took a step to his side and was half-standing in front of her. Again, if someone had done that even a month ago, she would've blown up and gotten pissed. She could take care of herself and made sure everyone knew it. But Jonathan protecting her? She was all over that. She actually liked it.

When Ian and Trent's fight brought them closer to where they were standing, Jonathan took hold of Kina's elbow and backed her up, while somehow still staying in front of her.

Jonathan wanted nothing more than to break up the fight, but since he wasn't a part of the show he couldn't. He knew Eddie would be beyond pissed if any of the staff cut in. Fighting was classic reality TV and usually brought huge audiences. Jonathan knew this wasn't cool and the men could really hurt each other. He caught Roger's eye. Roger was a teacher and probably had some experience in breaking up fights before. Jonathan gave him a chin-lift toward the two men.

Roger obviously got the gist of what Jonathan was trying to tell him. The staff of the show couldn't break up the fight, but the other contestants could. Roger grabbed Darius by the shoulder and the two of them made their way over to Trent and Ian who were still trying to pulverize the other. Benedict and Nash saw what they were doing and went over to help as well.

"Yo! Enough!" He tried to reason with them first. When it didn't even faze the two men slugging it out, Roger and Benedict grabbed Ian and Darius and Nash grabbed Trent. For a moment Kina couldn't see anything but elbows and fists. When the dust settled Trent was on the ground on his stomach and Ian was being held back with a man holding each arm.

"You, dick!" Ian yelled at Trent. "We could've won if you'd have just listened to me!"

"Whatever, Ian!" Trent returned. "If we'd gone

with your idea, we wouldn't even have made it as far as we did!"

"Enough!" Nash said loudly. "Geez. Just enough." He couldn't seem to come up with anything that would really convey his disgust with the other two men.

Kina looked at Eddie who was watching from the side with a look of glee in his eyes. An unplanned fight like this was reality show gold. Usually producers would have to ply their contestants with alcohol to get such a great fight. Not here. It was obvious he loved it. Kina shook her head. One more reason she didn't want to work for him anymore. He cared more about ratings than the people on his shows.

The trip back to the rendezvous point was quiet. When they pulled up to the shore everyone got out and went to their positions for the official ceremony. They all knew who'd be going home; it was just a matter of having it said officially for the show. After Shannel's speech Trent and Ian actually had to climb into the same van to be driven off the impromptu set. Kina could only chuckle at that. Given how pissed they were at each other, it had to be an interesting drive back to the production house to pack!

The rest of the contestants and Shannel were quickly hustled into another van and all of the camera crew got into their SUV to head back to their own hotel. They were looking forward to having the next day off. After their long three-day outdoor adventure, it'd be great to be able to sleep in and be lazy.

Chapter 10

Kina knew what she wanted to ask Jonathan, knew what she really wanted, but she was scared to death to actually ask. She knew it'd be up to her, he wouldn't bring it up. As they all gathered their camera equipment from the back of the SUV, she thought about the best way to bring it up.

Ah hell, there was no good way. He'd always been honest and up front with her, so there was no reason she shouldn't be the same way with him. She lagged behind the others, knowing Jonathan would hang back with her. He was never far from her side nowadays and she liked knowing he had her back.

Softly, as they walked towards the hotel, Kina said, "Would you rather sleep by yourself, or in the warm arms of a friend?"

Jonathan stopped in his tracks and stared down at Kina. *Holy crap, had she really just said that?* "Ask me," he demanded. He had to make sure she was serious and wasn't just playing their game with him.

Kina looked him right in the eyes and asked, "Do you want to sleep over tonight?"

"Hell yes, honey. I wanted to ask. I've gotten used to having you in my arms, but I didn't want to push. I told you that you'd be in charge and I was determined to make sure you knew I meant it. Thank you for wanting to be with me. Thank you for trusting me."

Kina smiled at Jonathan. God, it was heady to have this strong alpha man thank her for something so simple, as asking if he'd spend time with her.

"Let's get cleaned up and meet the others downstairs for some good, hot food. See you in about forty minutes?"

Kina smiled and nodded. "Thank you for not making this any weirder than it already feels."

He leaned down and kissed her temple. "Go get clean. I'll see you in a bit."

Jonathan smiled as he entered his room. He was thrilled Kina wanted to be with him. He hadn't lied to her. He'd slept better with her in his arms, than he had in the last couple of months, since Becky had been hurt. Jonathan debated not shaving off his three day beard, but in the end decided he liked to be able to feel Kina's soft skin on his face rather than have his scruffy whiskers get in the way. Eventually, when he had his way, he didn't want to scrape up her sensitive skin either.

Kina climbed into the shower and noticed in the bathroom mirror, the goofy grin she was wearing as she stepped in. God, had she ever been this giddy around a guy before? She didn't think so. There was something special about Jonathan, but she couldn't put her finger on it. He was so different from any man she'd ever been around before. He was sensitive and not afraid to put his own feelings out there, but at the same time he was as alpha as anyone she'd ever met. Alpha in a good way, not an asshole way like Matt was. He was quick to protect her and make sure no one gave her any crap. But he'd also let her do her own thing, as long as he was sure she wasn't in any danger. It was heady. She still had no idea where anything was going with them.

He was going back to Arizona in a few weeks and she had to decide what she was going to do. A part of her wanted nothing more than to drop everything and follow Jonathan, but the other, more independent part of her, didn't want to be one of those women who blindly followed a man. It was so confusing.

Jonathan and Kina met outside their rooms about forty minutes later. They were both showered and cleaned up. Jonathan leaned down and kissed Kina on the cheek. He lingered a bit and nuzzled the side of her neck, breathing in deeply.

"God, you smell good, honey."

"It's just soap."

"Yeah, but it's soap on you, so it smells like nothing I've ever smelled before."

Gah. See? He was awesome.

Jonathan grabbed her hand, as if he had no concerns about who'd see them holding hands, and led her down the hall to the small elevator. They were meeting the others in the hotel restaurant to have a hot meal.

Dinner was fun. They were all in great moods. The fight between Ian and Trent was interesting and everyone knew their camera work would make for great TV. Being warm and clean was also a very big boost to everyone's feeling of well-being.

Carl brought out his smart phone and started showing off pictures of his girls. Catherine was a very cute dark-haired five-year old. He related a story about Catherine getting home from her first day of all-day kindergarten a couple of months ago. When she arrived home she stood in the hallway with her hands on her hips and declared loudly, "You fooled me! School is hard!" Apparently, going from a part time day-care/preschool to an all-day kindergarten was tough for a little kid. Kina could almost picture the outrage on her little face.

Carl also told them all a story about a time when Celeste saw an old picture of John Lennon with colored eyeglasses and insisted she get a pair too. She was only six years old and the only kid in her elementary school to have blue-tinted glasses and according to Carl, she rocked them!

Not to be left out, Taylor got in the action. He bragged about his girls and tried to outdo Carl's stories. The funniest story was about Phyllis. They'd been hanging out at Taylor's mom's house and listening to old songs from the seventies. Phyllis was around six years old and loved singing and dancing. After a morning spent playing games and listening to music, Phyllis disappeared. When they found her, she was in the front yard of the little house, dancing all over and pretending she was on stage. She was belting out the words to *Shake Your Booty* by KC and the Sunshine Gang, as loud as she could. Taylor recalled the neighbors standing on their porches laughing hysterically and clapping for his little girl. She'd misunderstood the words to the song and had been entertaining the entire neighborhood by singing "Shake Your Booby" over and over. They still hadn't let her live it down.

Carl's other daughter, Beth, was adorable. She was tall and skinny and apparently, sometimes clueless. He gave an example of how, once when she was young, they were in a public restroom and Beth repeatedly was running her hands under the faucet at the sink to wash her hands. She looked up at Carl with tears in her eyes and said, "It's broken!" Carl leaned over and turned the knob. Beth had assumed it was an automatic faucet.

Kina laughed at the men's stories. It was obvious they were madly in love with their kids. She'd never been sure she even wanted kids, but listening to the two men talk about their families with such devotion and love made her wonder if she should re-think her decision. She didn't have a close-knit family growing up and never really knew families could be like this. Hell, she didn't really know how to be a mother. She'd learned how to be a hard worker from her mom, but any maternal instincts she had, were buried deep. Her dad, not being around, was also a factor. She wondered, for a moment, if her life would've been different if he'd been there. Would he have been protective of her, or only annoyed she was underfoot? She had no idea, but shrugged off the bad mood threatening. She couldn't change the past and besides, she'd turned out all right in the end.

Jonathan squeezed her hand. She looked up at him. He wasn't looking at her, but she knew he'd somehow felt her mood change. How had he gotten to be so perceptive?

After a couple of hours of good food and good company, they decided to call it a night. Kina didn't want it to be obvious that Jonathan would be sleeping in her room, but she also didn't really want to hide their relationship. She surprised herself with that thought. Relationship. Yes, she admitted to herself, she was in a relationship with Jonathan. It was different from anything she'd had before, and that made it more special.

She'd never had a relationship with a guy and not slept with him. She didn't sleep around, but she was also very cautious. She always kept men at arms' length emotionally, until she decided she was ready. Nothing about this relationship with Jonathan fit the pattern she normally followed. Mentally shrugging, she reflected that it was also, so far, the best relationship she'd ever had, so she might as well just go with it. She knew it was soon, but spending such close quarters with someone, day in and day out, had a way of speeding up relationships. She'd seen it over and over on the relationship shows she'd filmed. She supposed she and Jonathan were no different, really.

Kina had no idea whether they'd have sex tonight or not. She wanted it with him; there was no doubt about that. It was obvious they had sexual chemistry, but she was also enjoying the intimacy they had, without the pressure of sex to go with it.

As they neared their rooms, Carl and Taylor said good night and entered their rooms without looking back. Jeff put his hand on his doorknob and looked back at Jonathan and Kina. Jonathan had taken her hand again and was holding it as Kina dug the key to her room out of her back pocket. Jeff had been quiet; he hadn't made any snide remarks all night about the intimacy the two of them obviously shared. Kina braced herself. She figured he couldn't hold out forever. He had to make some sort of comment. She figured he'd burst if he didn't.

He surprised both of them by simply raising one eyebrow and then mock-saluting them as he entered his own room and closed the door.

Kina looked up at Jonathan and asked skeptically, "Do you think that's the end of that?"

"Frankly hon, I don't care. He can think whatever he wants, as long as he doesn't disrespect you."

Kina just shook her head. How the hell could he just get better and better?

"I'll give you some time to get ready. Half an hour okay? I'll come back over, if that'll work for you?"

Kina leaned up toward Jonathan. He was perfect. Seriously. "Sounds good."

She kissed his lips briefly then turned and opened her door. She smiled at him as she shut it softly behind her. The second it closed she whirled around to face her room. Oh my God! It was a mess! She hurriedly started throwing clothes into drawers and tidying up. She only had thirty minutes to make the room presentable and to figure out what she was going to wear to bed.

* * *

Exactly thirty minutes later, Kina heard a soft tap at the door. She smoothed her hands down the sleep shirt she was wearing. She didn't own anything sexy and figured he'd better get used to her like this. She'd never understood how people could sleep in long slinky nightgowns or even skimpy little tops. Both of those would annoy her to no end, while she was sleeping. Nightgowns tended to get twisted around her body and the sexy little tops were usually made with a lot of lace and other uncomfortable materials that would rub and irritate her skin all night.

A thought struck her for the first time. *Duh, maybe people didn't actually sleep in those things, they only wore them for their partner and then they came off and they slept nude.*

Kina opened the door and smiled shyly at Jonathan. How the hell did the man look sexy as hell in everything he wore? He was wearing a pair of sweat pants and a T-shirt that looked molded to his body. She stood back to let him enter her room. What was she doing? He was so out of her league. He'd said she was beautiful, but he was the beautiful one.

Jonathan could tell Kina was starting to freak out. She looked sexy as hell standing there in a huge T-shirt with her feet crossed over one another. He entered the room, closed the door behind him and turned, then took her face in his hands and leaned down, tilting her face up to his. He kissed her, keeping it light, even though he wanted nothing more than to throw her down on the bed behind her and strip her out of that shirt.

When he lifted his mouth from hers, he didn't let go of her face. He asked teasingly, "Would you rather sleep with an entire college basketball team or a chess team?" She laughed, as he'd meant her to. "Relax, Kina," he scolded her gently. "It's just me."

"That's what I'm nervous about," she answered, giggling nervously.

"Come here." Jonathan wrapped Kina up in his embrace. She fit against him perfectly. He just held her for a long moment. He let go, just enough for her to lean back to look up at him, but kept his hands clasped at her lower back.

"There's nothing I want more, than to strip you out of this sexy-as-all get-out shirt and make love to you all night long." At her nod he kept going, not letting her speak. "But I don't want to rush us. I know you're mine. I know I want you for a lot longer than a quick fling, while on location. I was serious the other night, when I told you I wanted you to come with me to Arizona. I won't bug you about it, but know that what's between us is more than just here and now. You're more than just some itch to scratch while I'm here. Whatever you need, I'm here. For now, can we just hang out, get to know each other better, watch some TV, and get a good night's sleep?"

Kina was speechless, probably for the first time in her life. It was like this man could reach right into her brain and pull out her innermost thoughts and desires. Yes, she wanted him. She wanted to see first-hand what was underneath the tight clothes he was wearing, but she also wanted to feel as if he wanted her for *her*, not just for her body.

"I'd like that," she told him with a smile. They made their way to the bed. Kina pulled back the covers and they crawled in. She nestled against him. Neither moved to turn on the television.

"Tell me about your family's animal refuge."

Jonathan spent the next ten minutes talking all about the coyotes they helped rescue and the work that went into the refuge, keeping the animals happy and healthy. Kina thought he was so lucky to have such great parents and such a great legacy in his family.

After a moment's silence Jonathan asked, "Would you rather have a perfect sense of direction or a perfect sense of time?"

After laughing and having a thorough debate on which would be better, Kina said, "I don't know if I've told you this or not, Jonathan, but I like you."

Jonathan gave her a squeeze. "Good. You know, I like you too."

As Kina fell asleep in his arms, she thought it was one of the best days she'd had in a long time.

Chapter 11

The next few days were crazy for the camera crew. Eddie had suddenly decided that he wanted the four men who were left on the show to be filmed practically all day, every day, which was ridiculous because they weren't *doing* anything at the production house. A schedule was worked out between the five camera operators, so that two of them would be at the house at all times. That meant long hours of work for all of them. Long, *boring* hours.

Kina tried not to be upset at not being able to sleep in Jonathan's arms. It was ridiculous. She'd been sleeping by herself for a long time now and she wasn't the type of person who needed to sleep in a man's arms in order to get a good night's rest. And while she was sleeping well at night because she was exhausted, a part of her, deep down, admitted to like being in Jonathan's arms at night. She worried about him. Was he still having nightmares? Was *he* sleeping all right? Gah. It was crazy. Of course, he was just fine. He was a guy. Guys slept with different women all the time. Right?

Kina tried to convince herself that was true of Jonathan as well, but she knew he was different. She wasn't sure how she knew, just that she did. They'd seen each other briefly in passing, one morning that week.

Jonathan was coming back from his shift at the house, just as Kina was headed out. He'd walked right up to her and clasped the back of her neck and brought her head to rest on his chest. He always did that. Hauled her against him with a hand behind her neck or head. She should hate it. She should protest it. But she didn't and couldn't feel the need to.

Jonathan hadn't said much, but she could feel every muscle in his body relax once she was in his arms.

"Are you okay?" she'd asked him quietly. "Are you sleeping all right? Any more nightmares?"

"I'd sleep better with you in my arms. No more nightmares. Thank you for being concerned about me. I don't think anyone I've ever dated, wanted to know about my well-being before. It means a lot to me, hon."

He kissed the daylights out of her, backed her up, kissed her forehead briefly, then said as a goodbye endearment, "Would you rather never get enough sleep, or sleep so much you're only awake for a few hours each day?"

Kina smiled. God, he was cute. "Get some sleep, Jonathan," she murmured, letting go of him and stepping back. "I'll see you soon."

"Be safe."

Those two words stayed with Kina the entire time it took to get to the house. He'd begun to tell her that when they separated. He didn't say, "Have a good day", or "I'll miss you," it was always, "Be safe." She figured it had something to do with Becky, but that wasn't all of it. He truly wanted her to be safe when he wasn't there with her, couldn't be there to protect her himself.

Today's shift promised to be another boring day. Unfortunately, Jeff was her camera wing-man for the day. To be fair, he'd been behaving himself recently, but

Kina had worked with him long enough to know there was no way he'd be able to control himself much longer. She knew he was bursting to say something snide and/or sexist to her.

Their shift in the house started out with the men sitting around eating breakfast. It was quite boring. Even the contestants themselves seemed bored out of their skulls.

It was Darius who came up with the bright idea of sneaking out of the house, which was surprising, since he was the stereotypical, serious chemist. Kina wouldn't have thought he had it in him to be such a rebel. But she supposed the 'Alaskan sickness' that sometimes came over the residents of Alaska in the winter didn't discriminate against those who were only visiting.

Knowing they had to take the cameras with them, the men decided to take the fifteen passenger van, instead of the small rental car Shannel and Eddie traveled in.

Kina rolled her eyes at the men. They were acting more like teenagers, who didn't want to get caught sneaking out after curfew than grown men.

She didn't particularly like the fact they were leaving the house, but what choice did she have? She'd just have to roll with the punches. She tried once to convince the men they shouldn't leave, but she was quickly overridden. They were on a mission. Even Jeff got in on the act and told her she was being a kill-joy and she should just go with it.

Benedict was voted to be the driver. Jeff sat in the front seat, filming the men while Kina sat in the back, off to the side, so she wouldn't be in Jeff's shot when he turned his camera around. They were driving around aimlessly. The guys had no idea where they were or what they wanted to do, they only knew they were 'free' for the moment.

Because Benedict was driving, he saw the strip club first. Of course the others enthusiastically agreed, it was the best idea to stop in for a while. Kina rolled her eyes again. Geez. Could they really want this little visit to be on national television for all to see? She knew Eddie would be pissed they'd left the house, but he'd still use the footage, especially if they did something dumb. And this was as dumb as they could get.

Benedict parked the monstrous van and everyone climbed out. It was ten in the morning, not exactly prime time for this type of establishment, but it was still open. Kina laughed to herself, knowing the types of women who would be dancing this early wouldn't be the best the place had to offer. Those women worked the night shift, where they could make more money when there were more customers.

The first issue materialized as soon as they walked inside. The manager came storming over, demanding the cameras be turned off. Kina couldn't blame him. The place was horrible. Even in the dim light the room she could see the tattered curtains, the worn and stained carpets, and the sad little stage where the strippers would dance. It smelled of stale cigarette and cigar smoke and something funky Kina couldn't place. One of the only good things about this venture was the fact that there were only two other customers in the place.

Jeff actually stepped up for once and calmed the manager down. He explained they were not from a documentary, or anything that would show his esteemed establishment in a negative light, but rather they were a reality show. He agreed they wouldn't film any of the women dancing, but only the men on the reality show.

Kina saw Jeff slip the sleazy manager a hundred dollar bill, which seemed to be what the guy was waiting for. Jerk.

The men got a table and enthusiastically ordered beers. Kina was disgusted. Beer wasn't her alcoholic drink of choice at any time, and certainly not so early in the morning. She tried to turn off the logical side of her brain and turn on her camera side. She had to get the men in the best light so the shots would be usable on TV. She couldn't use the light on her camera, that would ruin the ambiance of the shot.

For the next hour she and Jeff rotated around the table, filming the guys getting hammered and hitting on the waitresses. They hooted and hollered at the two strippers who occasionally took the stage for short, rather uninspired, pole dances. Finally, figuring she had enough shots of the men being idiots, she motioned to Jeff, that she was going to go outside for a break.

Being smart, she left the camera inside with Jeff. She wasn't going to risk bringing the expensive electronic equipment outside, in the rather questionable area of town, but she slipped outside into the fresh air.

It was still cold outside, but it felt great after the stifling atmosphere of the strip club. The cloying smell of perfume mixed with all the other disgusting smells was nauseating. Kina looked around. She knew Alaska was beautiful. She'd seen it firsthand on her outings with Jonathan and during filming of the show, but this street was not beautiful at all.

There was trash all around, as if no one cared about actually trying to put it in a garbage bin. There were plenty of used cigarettes strewn everywhere on the ground. She could just imagine the employees and customers alike stepping outside, smoking their cigarette down to the nub to get that last bit of nicotine before throwing it on the ground, stepping on it briefly, then disappearing back inside the dark building.

Kina looked up and down the street. There were a few other businesses, but they were all currently closed, except for the liquor store at the end of the road. There weren't many people around, but those that were had their heads down and were rushing from one place to another. There was a bus stop across from the strip club that had one rather unsavory looking character waiting for the next bus, at least that was what she assumed he was doing.

Kina was startled to see he was watching her. He was wearing black cargo pants and black boots, the kind she imagined soldiers wore. She couldn't see what type of shirt he was wearing as he had on a long black coat which was buttoned up to his chin. She shivered. She was a pretty worldly woman, and she'd lived in some pretty scary places growing up as a child, but this guy was bad news. Break-time was over. Kina slipped back inside the rundown building regretfully. Even with the creepy bus stop guy, she'd much rather be outside in the fresh air than in there.

For the first time since she'd arrived, she started to feel uncomfortable. She was truly on her own now. She saw Jeff had also put down his camera, and was doing shots with the guys. Unbelievable.

Kina marched over to the men. "What the hell, Jeff?"

He mocked her and responded, "What the hell, Kina?"

All the men thought that was the funniest thing they'd ever heard in their lives and erupted in laughter. Great. Just great.

She reached down and hauled Jeff up by the collar of his shirt. He wasn't expecting it and his arms pin wheeled as he tried to regain his balance. As the other men continued to laugh, Kina yanked Jeff away from the table toward the door. When they'd gotten far enough away so that the others couldn't hear them, she lit into him.

"Seriously? You know we aren't supposed to hang out with the contestants! And drinking this early in the morning? We have to get them out of here and back to the house!"

"Shut up, Kina. Serioushly," he slurred, "haf some fun for once. You're alwaysh so uptight. Have a drink with ush. Maybe then you can schow us what you're schowing Jon-boy."

Kina shoved Jeff away from her as hard as she could. Jesus, he was an ass. She left him standing by the door and wandered over to the bar. She hauled herself up on one of the stools and refused to look back at the table of idiot men. The bartender came over to where she was sitting.

"Can I get you anything?"

"I'd love a bottle of water, if you have one," Kina told her.

The bartender nodded and turned away to get the drink for her. When she returned, she asked Kina, "So, what's the deal?" and motioned with her head toward the table of idiots Kina had come in with.

Kina figured, at this point, she had nothing to lose. The bartender was surprisingly pretty. She didn't seem as worn down as the other women in the place. "Those idiots are on a reality show and busted loose from their leash today. As a part of the camera crew, I had no choice but to follow along. The other camera guy over there, is just an imbecile."

The bartender laughed. "Well, you just sit here as long as you need to. We'll just let them have their fun." She got serious and leaned over the bar toward Kina. "As long as they're in here, they'll be all right. They'll be poorer for it, but safe. But don't let them wander around outside when they leave. It's not a safe area for a bunch of drunk men who think they're invincible."

Kina nodded. "Yeah, I kinda got that in the five minutes I was standing outside, taking a break." She thought about calling Eddie, but figured the men would soon get bored and they'd be heading back to the production house.

Unbelievably, the men hung out at the strip club all afternoon. Food was scrounged up from somewhere to feed them and to help keep the alcohol flowing and their buzz continuing. Kina didn't bother filming anymore. It was pointless. When the place started getting more crowded, the bartender let Kina put both the cameras behind the bar, to keep them safe.

Kina considered calling Jonathan, but talked herself out of it. This wasn't his problem. She was an adult and a professional, she could handle it. All she had to do was get the drunks back to the van and back to the house. Easy.

* * *

Not so easy. First, the men didn't want to leave. Kina supposed she couldn't blame them. The strippers that had come in for the second shift were much better-looking than the ones who had been working when they'd arrived. Second, they were so drunk they couldn't think clearly. And third, they knew what awaited them back on the set. Boredom, and most likely they'd be in trouble for sneaking out.

Finally after around seven hours in the bar, Kina had enough. They were leaving. She considered leaving them all there, but knew that wasn't cool and they'd only get in more trouble, if she left. She begged the new manager on duty to help her get all of the men to the van. Reluctantly he agreed, after all, they'd been spending a lot of money all day and he didn't want to lose his best customers.

Kina had to stand and wait for each of the men to say goodbye to their waitresses and the dancers they'd been feeding money to all day. Kina rolled her eyes for what seemed like the hundredth time that day. She watched as they groped the women's breasts and slapped their asses for good measure. Good God, they were pathetic. The waitresses just laughed, knowing they'd made a boatload of money off the group. 'Extreme Alaskan', Kina's ass, more like 'Pathetic Losers.'

The group stumbled toward the van, laughing loudly and exclaiming that the day had been the 'best ever' and how they'd all be best friends forever. They were acting just like drunk college women. Kina and the manager somehow were able to get all the men inside the van safely. At least they were happy drunks. It would've been worse if they'd been mad or angry when drunk.

At the last minute Kina remembered their cameras. Crap. It was a good thing she hadn't left them at the bar. That would've meant another trip back to this awful part of town to retrieve them.

"Can you please stay here for just a minute and watch them to make sure they don't do anything stupid?" she pleaded with the manager. She didn't want to leave them there for even the two minutes it'd take her to run back inside and grab the cameras. Thank God, she had the keys to the van in her pocket. At least they couldn't drive drunk or leave her there stranded.

When it looked like he was going to decline, Kina sighed and reached into her pocket and brought out a twenty. "Would this help convince you?"

Smirking, the manger pocketed the money and said, "This'll hold me for five minutes. Better hurry, sweet cheeks."

Ugh. Another jerk, in the long line of jerks, she'd had to deal with that day. Running back into the building she'd hoped never to have to enter again, she rushed over the bar. The bartender saw her coming and lifted the little wooden door, granting her access to the area behind the bar.

"Thanks Shirley, appreciate it. Have a good night."

She and Shirley had gotten on a first name basis since Kina had been there all day, and she waved as Kina backed out of the bar area with a camera in each hand and headed back toward the front door.

Stepping back outside was like sucking in oxygen, after being underwater for too long. Even though the area of town they were in was crappy, the air smelled fresh and sweet. She loved Alaska for that fact alone. Kina fast walked toward the van. She could hear the men inside singing a song about a lumberjack. She smiled, thinking how ridiculous the entire situation was. She only had to deal with the drunken louts for another half an hour or so, then she'd be free.

She should've been paying attention to her surroundings and not thinking about the warm bath she wanted to take that night. Kina suddenly found herself sprawled on the ground, looking up at two men. They were tall, but not very muscular and they smelled horrible. Kina could smell them from her position on the dirty ground. They smelled like body odor and pee. Gross. She didn't have the time or the patience for this. All she wanted to do was get back to the hotel and get clean and sleep. She sighed.

Kina hoped the cameras weren't broken. She'd taken a hard tumble and had both hands full with the cameras so she couldn't break her fall. One of the guys had shoved her hard from behind. She picked herself up off the ground and faced the men. She glanced quickly at the van, although she could still hear the drunken singing coming from the men, they weren't paying any attention to her.

"You don't want to do this," she told the thugs honestly, knowing she could kick their butts. She hadn't had self-defense training for nothing. Although typically, in self-defense one was supposed to do just enough to get away, she had to get to the van and get out of there. These guys wouldn't let her calmly open the van door and start up the engine nonchalantly. She had to convince them she wasn't a pushover and to leave her alone.

"Hand over the cameras," the taller of the two men growled.

"Like hell," Kina answered, not thinking.

"Hand 'em over," the second man growled, not expanding on his threat.

Kina didn't wait to hear anything else. She'd learned in her classes to use every body part she had to hurt the other person. Her head, her elbows, her knees, her feet. As the first man came toward her, she aimed her foot at his knee. She figured most men would think a woman would go for their family jewels first, so she aimed for another basic pressure point. She kicked him as hard as she could, not holding back in the slightest. Sure enough, as soon as her foot made contact with his knee, he went down, hard.

Seeing his buddy rolling around on the ground seemed to galvanize the other guy. He roared and grabbed Kina from behind. Kina took a deep breath, turned her head to the side and slipped right out of his hold, just like she'd practiced in class. He was so surprised at her quick escape, he didn't manage to block the heel of her hand as it slammed into the fleshy part of his face. He howled in pain and staggered away from her. He blindly swung his fist in her direction and before Kina could duck, managed to nail her in the cheek.

Damn, that hurt. Holy crap. Getting hit in the face hurt. She'd never been hit before. On television, actors always made it look like it wasn't that painful. Shit. She'd had no idea how much it would hurt. She blinked hard. She couldn't break down now.

Kina ignored her throbbing cheek for the moment and reached down to grab the cameras and get the hell out of there. Before she could reach the damn equipment and head for the van, the first guy was on his feet again. Kina sighed. She was done with this, dammit.

He grabbed Kina's wrist and said confidently, "Try getting away now, bitch."

Really? He thought holding her by her wrist was keeping her secure? That was the easiest hold to get out of, if someone grabbed you. Kina looked down and yanked her arm towards herself, right where his thumbs and fingers met. It was like slicing butter with a warm knife, her wrist came free so easily. She brought her knee up quickly and slammed it into his groin this time.

He fell to the ground, swearing profusely.

She turned and delivered a roundhouse kick to the other guy who'd recovered and was coming at her. She hit him right in the femoral artery, which worked just as well as nailing him in the groin. He went down hard.

Not waiting for either of them to recover again, she snatched the cameras up and headed for the van at a dead run. Damn the other guys for not being sober enough to be aware of what was going on and come help her. And *double* damn that manager. He was leaning against the van watching her. *Watching*. Bastard. He hadn't bothered to come to her aid.

Kina briefly thought about Jonathan and how there was no way he'd simply stand against a van and watch a woman, or anyone, fight. He'd be right there helping. It wouldn't matter if he knew the people in the fight. She couldn't think about him right now. She had to concentrate on getting out of there.

She snarled at the manager as he strolled away, but didn't bother wasting any energy on bitching him out. She didn't have the time. She practically threw the cameras into the van and vaulted up into the driver's seat. She ignored the comments from the guys, who still had no idea what had just happened right in front of their damn faces, and jammed the key into the ignition. She cranked the engine over and slammed the gearshift into drive. She watched as the two thugs in the parking lot came toward the van, albeit slow, because of the injuries she'd inflicted on them, but coming toward her nonetheless.

She slammed her foot on the gas and everyone in the van was thrown backward in their seats. Again, she ignored the drunken comments from the men and concentrated on getting out of the parking lot, without flipping the van. She enjoyed watching the thugs leap out of the way. She would've hit them without a second thought if they hadn't moved. Assholes.

The back end of the van fishtailed as she turned onto the street. She regained control of the van and let out a sigh. Holy crap. That wasn't fun. She reached a hand up to her face. She realized she was shaking, most likely from adrenaline. Her face also hurt. She figured she'd most likely have a black eye as well. That guy had gotten her pretty good when he'd hit her. She blinked her eyes rapidly, to keep the tears that were welling from falling. She wouldn't fall apart. She wouldn't fall apart. She wouldn't fall apart.

"Wooooooo, Kina, you're Mario An-An-An…whatever hish name ish," Nash drunkenly slurred from the backseat.

"You go, grrrrrrl!"

"Shit, I hit my head."

Kina ignored the comments, concentrating on figuring out how to get back to the production house. Since Benedict had driven them out she wasn't exactly sure as to how he'd gotten them to the strip club in the first place. After driving around for a bit she recognized one of the main roads she'd been on with Jonathan and turned.

Jeff was surprisingly quiet, sitting in the front seat next to her. After what seemed like hours, but was probably only around twenty minutes, Kina pulled into the driveway of the production house. Eddie wrenched open the front door and stalked toward the van. Kina almost wanted to laugh at the look on his face, when the four contestants tumbled out of the van toward the house. At this moment, in their shared drunkenness, they were the best of friends. Any disagreement they'd had in the past were only memories.

"Where the hell have you been?" Eddie demanded of the group of drunks.

"Schrip Club." Darius slurred, not hiding anything. "It was aweshome!"

The others added their agreement and continued into the house, laughing and giggling like little girls.

Kina turned off the van and grabbed her camera that was lying precariously between the front two seats. She left Jeff's for him. She'd had enough of covering his butt for the day. She stepped down out of the van and headed toward the SUV to put her camera up.

"Where the hell do you think you're going?" Eddie scowled at her. Since he didn't have the men to yell at anymore, he changed his target to her. "Why the hell did you take these guys out without my permission?"

"I'm putting my camera up, then I'm going to go back to the hotel," she said without turning around. She'd had enough of annoying men for the day.

Eddie had come up behind her without her noticing and he grabbed her bicep and tried to turn her around to look at him.

Kina ripped her arm out of his grasp and whirled around to face him. "Keep your hands off me, Eddie. I've had a hell of a day babysitting your actors and Jeff. I don't want to talk to you; I don't want to look at Jeff. All I want to do is go back to the hotel and take a shower. You got a problem with that?"

Looking uncomfortable, Eddie stared at Kina's face, noticing for the first time the bruise on her face. "Uh, are you all right?" he said awkwardly and belatedly.

"I'm fine," Kina said shortly turning back around to place the camera in the SUV.

"Jeff," she called out. "I'll be in the car. Do whatever you have to do and I'll wait for you, but I'll only wait for five minutes. After that you're spending the night here."

Eddie turned to lambast Jeff, wanting to yell at someone, only to watch as Jeff stumbled as he climbed out of the van and tripped over his own feet. Kina and Eddie stared at the man, now lying in the dirt, as he laughed uncontrollably over his clumsiness. Kina sighed, and ignoring the man trying to climb to his feet, went back to the van and grabbed Jeff's camera. If she didn't take it with her, it would sit in the van all night. Jeff was in no shape to even remember he *was* a cameraman, much less remember to pick up the camera and bring it with him.

On her way back toward the SUV, she said, "Eddie, help him into the backseat. I'll take him back to the hotel and get the tapes from today back to you tomorrow."

Eddie, knowing by the look on her face that she was at the end of her rope for the day, amazingly did as she asked. He stood back after he'd closed the door on his drunk cameraman and watched as Kina pulled away from the house without looking back.

Chapter 12

Kina pulled up to the hotel, dreading trying to get a drunk Jeff up to his room. As soon as she pulled into the parking lot, she saw Jonathan waiting for her. Crap. She had no idea how he knew when they'd be back, but maybe he had just been hanging out in the lobby waiting for her. On one hand, she was glad he was there so she didn't have to deal with Jeff on her own, but on the other hand she knew he was going to lose his shit over her face.

She'd checked it out in the car mirror before she left the production house. She was right, she had the beginnings of a black eye and the cheek would definitely bruise. Luckily, the guy hadn't hit her nose. The last thing she wanted was to deal with was a broken nose. She didn't think she needed to go to the hospital, nothing was broken, she'd just be sore for a while. It definitely could've been a lot worse. All in all, she'd been lucky.

She parked the car and rested her head on the steering wheel for just a moment. That moment was long enough for Jonathan to open her door. She raised her head and turned to look at him. She knew the moment he realized something was wrong. The look in his eyes turned from gentle and welcoming to hard and angry.

"What the hell?"

Kina held her hand up and closed her eyes. "Can this wait?"

"Hell, no!" She felt his hand brush against her bruised face lightly. "Talk to me."

"Can we please get him to his room, first?"

Jonathan looked in the back seat at Jeff, who'd finally passed out on their way to the hotel. "No. I need to take care of you first. He can wait here," he told Kina resolutely.

"I'm fine, Jonathan; we have to get him upstairs."

Since the SUV had high seats, Jonathan was able to block her from getting out of the driver's seat simply by stepping closer to her. "What happened?" he said, holding on to his temper, by sheer force of will. "Tell me."

Kina sighed. She decided to give him the condensed version so they could get out of the parking lot. She also needed his touch, to feel connected, so she leaned her forehead against his chest, and grabbed hold of his T-shirt at his waist. She needed the connection with him, even if he would be mad at what she told him.

"The guys decided they were bored and wanted to go out. Since we were tasked with filming them, we went too. They found a strip club and spent the day drinking and having fun. On the way out of the joint, I was asked to give up the cameras. When I declined, they tried to convince me. I beat the crap out of them, we left, and here I am."

Jonathan had so many questions racing through his mind, he almost couldn't decide where to start. He stroked her hair from the top of her head down to the middle of her back where it ended, then brought his hand back up to her head to do it again. "Where were the guys when those thugs tried to convince you to give up the cameras?"

"In the van."

"Did they see what was going on?"

"I have no idea."

"Give me the keys."

Kina was startled by his request. She raised her head and looked at his face. What did he think he was going to do? "Uh, no."

Jonathan held out his hand again. "It wasn't a request, give me the keys."

"No, Jonathan. I don't know where you think you're going, but, just, no."

Jonathan leaned in close to Kina. "You don't get it. They should've taken care of you. You never should've been in that position."

"You're right, I shouldn't have been." Kina tried to reason with him. "But I was. And you know what? I took care of it myself. Just like I've been doing for most of my life."

"No, *you* don't get it. You're mine, now. If someone doesn't treat you the way you should be treated, it's my job to take care of it."

Kina was pissed now. "No, it's not. Geez, Jonathan, I can take care of myself. Look at me! I took on two grown men and I'm just fine. They're hurting more than I am!"

Jonathan was still pissed, but his hand was gentle as he cupped her cheek and ran his thumb over her bruised cheek. "No, you're not fine. They touched you. They never should have touched you. They hurt you. I'm just going to have a word with the men at the production house and explain."

"No!" Kina yelled, smacking his hand away from

her face and not wanting his gentleness while he stood there and metaphorically beat his chest like a caveman.

"You're not! Listen to me, Jonathan. You can't do this. I can't be with you if you're going to do this. What are you going to do when I trip over my own feet? Beat the crap out of someone standing next to me? What if someone accidentally elbows me in a store? You gonna knock them off their feet, yell at them? It's ridiculous. You knew I could take care of myself before you met me. What makes you think now is any different? You're acting like Matt. He used to beat the crap out of people he imagined looked at what was his too."

Jonathan tried to tamp down the hurt and fury her words caused him. "You're shaking, honey. You're hurt. I can't ignore that and not do anything."

"It's the adrenaline, Jonathan. I'm fine. Seriously. All I want to do is go upstairs and take a shower and lie down."

"Give me the keys and you can go and do that. I'll be back later."

Kina couldn't think of anything else to say. He wasn't hearing her. He was going to do what he wanted to do, just as Matt always did. She'd thought he was different. It was breaking her heart, to know he wasn't. She simply handed him the keys and waited for him to get out of the way. When he finally stepped back she jumped down and opened the back door. She got the cameras out of the back.

"Will you please help Jeff up to his room before you go?"

Without waiting for his answer, she turned toward the hotel doors.

"I'll let you know when I'm back and maybe we can get something to eat?"

Kina ignored him and entered the hotel without looking back, the tears coursing down her cheeks blinding her.

* * *

Jonathan knew Kina was pissed and upset, but she was asking too much of him to ignore what had happened to her. He was damn proud of her for being able to get herself out of the situation, but she shouldn't have *had* to do it. And that was the crux of the matter. The other men were right there and were too drunk to help her. She could've really been hurt.

He wanted to be with her, to help her clean up and take care of her face, but it was more important to him to go to the production house. He had to talk to the men. They had to know what they'd done. After Jonathan was done with them they wouldn't let a woman face two thugs on her own again, that was for sure.

After dragging Jeff up to his room and leaving him passed out on his bed, he drove to the production house. Eddie and Shannel weren't around anywhere. He went up the stairs to find the men still on the show. He'd teach them a lesson on how women should be treated that they'd never forget.

* * *

Kina heard Jonathan knocking on her door. She ignored him. She was broken by his refusing to listen to her. She knew he was an alpha and felt the need to be protective of her, but she'd begged him to let it go and he didn't. She wasn't sure she could spend her life with him watching over her like that, ignoring her wishes.

She couldn't go through it again. It had taken her months to get over the pain Matt had inflicted on her, she wasn't sure she'd ever get over it from Jonathan.

Jonathan knew Kina was in her room. She was obviously pissed at him. She couldn't seriously think he'd just leave it alone. No man in his right mind would ignore what happened if it had happened to his woman. He thought about what his brother would've done if this was Becky. He'd have lost his ever-loving mind. The only reason the two men who attacked his wife were still alive and breathing was because the police caught them before Dean did.

"Please let me in, Kina," Jonathan said softly at her door.

Kina bit her lip. It took everything she had to not answer him. He sounded so sad, but she couldn't give in. He'd hurt her. No, he'd devastated her.

"Did you get some ice for your face?"

God, why did he have to be so concerned and so darn *nice*?

When she still didn't answer him, after a while she finally she heard him say, "Okay, I'm right next door, hon. If you feel like talking later, please don't hesitate to come over. I'll see you tomorrow."

She turned her face into her pillow so he wouldn't hear her cry. She was so disappointed in him. She'd had such high hopes for their relationship and now she didn't know if she'd be able to trust him again the same way she had before this.

* * *

The tension in the SUV was ratcheted high the next morning on the way to the production set. Kina had skipped breakfast so she didn't have to talk to Jonathan. She knew he was waiting for her and wanted to talk to her, because he'd stopped by her door on his way down to breakfast.

"Kina? Are you awake? I'd like to talk to you before breakfast."

When she didn't answer, she'd heard him sigh. "Okay, you're still mad at me. You know what happened to Becky. I couldn't let this go. If the same thing happened to you, I'd lose it. I wouldn't be able to handle it. I'd hoped to be able to talk to you and explain what happened when I went over to the house yesterday." When she didn't answer him after several moments, he said, "I'll talk to you downstairs."

Kina sat fully dressed on her bed and listened to him walk away. She'd started to second-guess herself. Was she overreacting? His bringing up Becky's experiences had made her think. She knew how devastated Jonathan had been when Becky had been hurt. She *knew.* He'd opened himself up to her and told her everything. Had yesterday brought on flashbacks for him? Did he sleep all right last night? Oh, crap. She had a bad feeling she'd done him a disservice. She hung her head and closed her eyes. This was too hard. This was why she wasn't good at relationships. Knowing she had to face him at some point, she took a deep breath and made her way downstairs.

Jeff obviously wasn't feeling well that morning. He was hung-over and hurting. Kina didn't have any sympathy for him. He'd definitely overstepped his bounds as a camera operator yesterday. She wondered for a moment if he'd regretted it, then decided he probably didn't. For the first time since they'd gotten to Alaska, there was silence in the car on the way to the set. Taylor and Carl had no idea what was going on, but with the bruises on her face, they knew something was up. They stayed silent, but gave her concerned looks as they traveled toward the set.

Eddie was there to greet the SUV as they pulled up to the house. As soon as Jeff stepped out of the vehicle, Eddie asked to speak with him. Kina, Taylor, and Carl looked over at them with curiosity, but Kina noticed that Jonathan seemed to be ignoring them altogether. Eddie and Jeff were still talking, as the four of them walked into the house.

Not too long after that, Eddie entered the production house and closed the door. "Jeff won't be joining us on the rest of the show. It'll be up to the four of you to cover the rest of the competitions and to finish the filming. I understand, Kina, that what happened yesterday wasn't your fault, but I do expect in the future that if something like this happens again, you'll notify me immediately. You shouldn't have been put in that position and the men shouldn't have left the house, no matter how bored they were."

Kina could only nod. She was shocked. She'd never thought Eddie would've been that cool about the entire situation. If anything, she figured he'd be a jerk about it and cither fire her or at the very least scold her. It was hard for her to believe he'd actually fired Jeff. Why had he fired Jeff and not her? It didn't make any sense.

She looked sideways at Jonathan, he wouldn't meet her eyes. Hmm. She wondered if he had anything to do with it. Maybe she should've talked to him this morning, after all. She looked at Jonathan carefully for the first time that morning.

He had no outward cuts or bruises that would indicate he'd gotten in a fight the night before. That didn't necessarily mean anything, though. The other four guys were pretty drunk and they most likely couldn't defend themselves very well.

She looked at Jonathan's hands. If he'd decked any of the men, his knuckles would be bearing the marks. Nothing. They were as smooth as they had been the last time she'd seen him.

Eddie continued talking to the camera crew. "As you know, there are four contestants left. We'll begin having single-elimination contests from here on out. We'll obviously have two more competitions before the final event. The single eliminations will be handled with short challenges, and the final, for the 'Extreme Alaskan' title, will be another overnight assignment. I'll explain what that is when we get to it. In the meantime, I'll assign each of you to film one of the men. Stick with them, film everything they do. After recording today, I expect you all to check out of the hotel and stay here. The pressure will be on and I want to get all of their reactions on film. If you have any problems with that, you can talk to me later, but I expect that no one will. You're all professionals here, make sure you act like it."

Kina winced, knowing he wasn't really talking to her, but feeling bad all the same. She knew she should've called Eddie yesterday as soon as the men said they wanted to get out of the house, but she hadn't.

Kina caught the sympathetic look in Jonathan's eyes and looked away. She wasn't ready to deal with him. She knew he'd done something, but couldn't figure out what.

Jonathan was frustrated that he hadn't been able to tend Kina's face the night before. She was too pissed at him to let him into her room. He would've made sure she kept ice on it and hopefully that would've lessened the pain and the bruising. He hated that she had to take care of herself, but he'd had to go to the production house the night before. He just had to.

Jonathan winced at the condition of the four contestants as they entered the room after all the cameras were set up. They looked extremely hung-over and uncomfortable. He didn't have much sympathy for them, but he could still feel for them.

Jonathan thought back to the night before. He'd wanted to stay with Kina, but he couldn't. He had to protect her from anything like that ever happening again, on this show. The men had to know what they'd done and what their lack of action had done.

He hadn't fought anyone, that wasn't his style. But he'd slain them with his words. He made sure they knew what *could* have happened to Kina. He explained in great detail what a woman goes through when she's raped. What it does to their self-esteem and what kind of life they had afterward. He made them think about their moms and sisters and friends. Would they sit around and watch as someone precious to them fought for her life or fought to protect herself?

He'd ground them into dust with his words. He knew they'd never do it again, and that was what he was going for. He'd also sat down with Eddie and let him know all about the issues he and Kina had with Jeff. It wasn't that he was a bad worker or necessarily a bad person, but the chip on his shoulder was huge and the night before had been the last straw for Jonathan.

Eddie reassured him that he'd take care of the issue and Jonathan was glad to see this morning that the man had dealt with it. Jonathan had wanted to talk with Kina before breakfast and let her know what he'd done and how he'd dealt with had happened to her, but she wouldn't talk to him. It disappointed him, but he supposed he couldn't blame her. She'd been burnt before, by a man who'd taken over and acted way too macho and controlling. He'd just have to give her time, she'd come to him when she was ready…he hoped.

Kina watched, with no sympathy, as the four men competed in the next competition. They were all miserable, but she couldn't care less at the moment. Her face still hurt from the blow she'd taken the day before. She also knew she was sporting a nice bruise as well. She didn't bother to try to hide it with makeup. She wanted them to see what had happened to her. The pain wasn't anything that would keep her off the set and not working, but she still knew it was there nonetheless. None of the men would really look at her after seeing her black eye for the first time. She again wondered what Jonathan had said to them yesterday.

None of the four men looked like they'd been beaten up, at least from what Kina could see. It just didn't make sense to her. She knew Jonathan had been over to the house last night, but she couldn't fathom him just sitting down for a chat. Then again, that apparently seemed to have been just what happened. Crap. She'd expected him to beat the hell out of the men, that was what Matt would've done. She thought about how she'd obviously misjudged Jonathan…again.

Kina knew the competition today was geared towards punishing the men. Eddie was good at coming up with things like that. As he had Shannel explain, part of living in Alaska was being able to be self-sufficient. They were brought to a local homestead in the middle of nowhere. The owners, Mr. and Mrs. Morrell, had a pretty big farming operation, as well as an extensive garden. They were completely self-sufficient during the winter and had fresh eggs, milk, and enough vegetables to last them throughout the harsh season. They'd spent the entire summer working on killing enough game to freeze and growing the fresh food in their gardens.

Thank God, Eddie wasn't going to have them go out and hunt for anything. Kina knew someone would probably have blown off a foot or something, if they had to actually shoot live animals for the competition.

It seemed that today's challenge would be to milk a cow and fill an entire bucket with milk, gather a dozen eggs, behead a chicken, and pull weeds out of a section of the garden. It didn't seem that hard of a challenge, but with all of the men being hung-over, it'd be tough.

Kina was in charge of filming Darius. Overall, she found her attention wandering throughout the challenge. She kept thinking about Jonathan. She had been so mad at him last night; mad enough to never want to talk to him again, but now she was second-guessing herself. He'd been so calm this morning, saying he wanted to talk to her. He hadn't even tried to get her alone today. He was giving her space. She didn't know if she should be upset about that or not.

In her experience, men would try to get her to listen to them and didn't care if she wanted space or not. They just barged their way in and made her listen to what they had to say. Jonathan wasn't like that. He was giving her space, space she wasn't sure she wanted anymore. Oh, she figured she'd talk to him before the day was out, but for now she couldn't think about him and do her job.

She focused on Darius as he chased a chicken around a pen. He had to catch the thing then bring it to the block of wood they were using as a chopping block and cut its head off. Kina didn't even want to watch it through the lens of her camera; she couldn't imagine what the men felt like, actually doing it. The worst thing about it was the chicken running around without a head after the axe had been used. Kina always thought that was just a saying, 'running around like a chicken with its head cut off', but it was apparently true… Gross.

The competition was a timed one, as all of the men were expected to finish all of the tasks. The slowest man to finish would be the one to leave. Kina swore the men were deliberately trying to throw the competition. What did it say for your show when no one wanted to stay and they all wanted to be kicked off?

Kina watched the other men with only half an eye. She barely noticed when Roger went off into the bushes to throw up, after watching Nash cut the head off the chicken and get sprayed from head to foot, with its warm blood.

Finally, the torturous day was over. All four of the men had finished the tasks. Shannel and Eddie lined the men up next to the pen which held the cows. Now they had to stand there and smell the cow manure and wait for Shannel to finish with her speech. Kina swore the hostess made it extra-long on purpose. Finally, she was done and it was time to name the slowest competitor for the day. Benedict had completed all of the tasks the slowest and would be leaving the show. Kina tried not to laugh at the look of relief that crossed his face. Even funnier was the looks on Roger, Darius, and Nash's face when they realized they'd be staying for at least one more competition.

The ride back to the production house was quiet. Everyone except for Eddie and Shannel were now traveling in the same van, since they'd all fit.

Kina put her head on the seat behind her and closed her eyes. She was tired. Tired of trying to figure out where she and Jonathan stood, and honestly just tired of the whole camera operator gig. She never thought she'd feel that way. She remembered how much of a high it used to give her and the way she'd loved moving from show to show and getting the best shots. She thought about the joy she felt, watching the shows she'd worked on when they aired on television, recognizing her filming, being able to tell it apart from that of the other camera operators.

Now she never watched them. She'd lost the excitement she'd used to feel about her job. That made her sad. She felt lost. If she couldn't do this, what could she do?

Nash's words broke the silence in the van.

"I'm really sorry, Kina. We shouldn't have broken the rules, but more importantly we shouldn't have dragged you along to that shithole."

Darius chimed in when Nash quit talking. "We had no idea what was going on. We wouldn't have left you to deal with those assholes if we weren't so drunk. I know it's not an excuse, but we're sorry."

Kina expected it and wasn't surprised when Roger added his apology to the others'. "We hope you can forgive us, Kina. We were stupid and you paid the price."

The mood was solemn in the van until Nash broke the tension. "Although, we heard you kicked their asses."

Kina smiled. She *had* kicked their butts. She just wanted this all to be done. She didn't want them to keep bringing it up. She couldn't lie; she was glad they were sorry and that they'd apologized. Hopefully they'd learn from it, but she also wanted it done.

"It's okay, guys. I know how stir crazy it can be, cooped up in the production house. If you ever do anything like that again, I'll bring out the pictures I took of you all with those skanky strippers."

At their horrified looks, she let them off the hook. "Kidding. But you'd better hope Eddie doesn't want to use the footage we *did* take before the day got too crazy."

Everyone got out of the van after arriving at the house. Privacy was at a premium since everyone was now staying at the set. Kina knew she had to talk to Jonathan. He'd been quiet, too quiet. She didn't like it. She'd prefer him to be talking to her and joking. She missed it and she didn't like the awkwardness that surrounded them both.

"Can I talk to you, Jonathan?" she asked as they walked towards the house, honestly, not knowing what he'd say.

"Of course, Kina." She should've known he wouldn't play games with her.

"My room, after we get our cameras put away?" Since she was the only woman on the crew she had her own room. The guys all had to share a room. It was the only place she could think of that was guaranteed to be private. She desperately wanted things back the way they were between them, but wasn't sure how to get them there.

* * *

Jonathan took a deep breath. Thank God, she was going to talk to him. The day had been torture. He was glad the men had apologized. He knew he'd guilted them into it last night, but it was the right thing to do. He just hoped he could get Kina to listen to him, because he'd never be able to sit back and let her get hurt or disparaged and not do something about it. It'd be a change for her, but that's just the way it was. He couldn't change the person he was, just as he didn't want to change who she was.

He knocked on Kina's door about ten minutes later. He opened it when he heard her call for him to enter.

Kina was sitting on the edge of the bed looking uncomfortable. He opened his month to say something, he wasn't sure what, when she beat him to it.

"I'm sorry, Jonathan. I was out of line."

He shook his head. "No, you really weren't. I don't want you thinking you can't disagree with me. There'll be times when we don't agree, hon. Hell, I love that you can stand up to me. I don't ever want you to think that you can't. I'd even venture to guess we'll probably disagree a lot. You're passionate and I love that about you." When Kina opened her mouth to say something, he interrupted her again.

"But, you have to understand the way I am. I *know* you can take care of yourself, if you couldn't, you'd most likely be in the hospital because those guys would've done unspeakable things to you. But you don't *have* to do it all by yourself anymore. I know you're independent and strong as hell, but that doesn't mean I won't protect you. I still don't think you understand this yet, but you're mine. No one disrespects you and gets away with it. Let that sink in. I told you before and I'll keep saying it, until it sinks in."

He watched Kina as she sagged back on the bed. He stared at her, willing her to understand.

"When I was with Matt, we went out one time to have dinner. The waiter was cute and was harmlessly flirting with me. Matt didn't like it. He yelled at me all the way home, about how I was acting like a whore and didn't I know I was his? When we got home, he said he was going out and would be back. When he got home later that night, it was obvious he'd been in a fight. I found out later he went back to the restaurant and waited for that waiter to get off work. He beat the hell out of him right there in the parking lot, just to prove to himself that I was his and that no one flirted with his property. It embarrassed the hell out of me and I felt so bad for that poor waiter. He hadn't done anything wrong. It made me feel like I'd done something wrong, when I hadn't. It also made me realize I never wanted to be in a relationship like that again."

As much as he hated to hear her story, he got it. "I didn't touch them, Kina."

"I know. I figured that out, but I didn't know that this morning when you wanted to talk. I should've known you weren't like Matt, but I was stuck in the past. I heard you call me 'yours' and I was afraid you'd be like him. I'm sorry, Jonathan. I know you aren't like him. I do. I swear."

Jonathan walked over to Kina and knelt in front of her. He took her hands in his and stared up at her. "I'm not like him, hon. But you have to know, I'll protect you with my life if I have to. I want to stand next to you, not in front of you, but again, if I need to, I'll shove you behind me so fast, you won't know what hit you. If you want to flirt with a waiter, go for it. It's not going to make me lose control. I'll just know at the end of the night, you're going home with me, and you'll be in my bed. In fact, I encourage you to flirt with whoever you want, just know any time you do, I'll find a way to remind you that you're mine, while you're flirting." He smiled at her, imagining running his fingers up her thigh under the table while she smiled at a waiter.

He got serious again and repeated what he'd just told her. "I didn't touch them last night, Kina. I made it very clear that what they did was seriously messed up. They weren't too happy with me, but they understood where I was coming from. They were mortified about what happened to you and what could've happened to you. They had no idea what you went through and I think that was what finally got to them the most."

"What about Jeff?"

He sighed. He figured this was coming. "I had a talk with Eddie as well." He put his finger to her lips, knowing she'd protest. "Listen, please. Jeff had it coming. You know it as well as I do. He wasn't fired for good. I just explained to Eddie, how Jeff had no respect for any woman. That he wasn't good for the camaraderie of the camera crew. Since it's the end of the show and he didn't really need him, Eddie agreed to move him off the show. I should've shared this with you before I did it, but I saw red when I saw you'd been hurt and I hadn't been there. Not only did Jeff not do anything about it, but he'd joined the other idiots in getting hammered. It wasn't cool of him and although on some level, it wasn't cool of me to do what I did, again, I couldn't just let it go. I hope you understand."

He held his breath until Kina nodded. She opened her lips and licked his finger still resting there. Jonathan moaned, actually moaned. God, she was so sexy and holding himself back from her was killing him.

Kina smiled. She knew they had more to talk about. She was putting off having the conversation about what she was going to do after the show was over. She desperately wanted to let him know she'd come to Arizona with him, but she was scared. She wasn't one hundred percent sure it was what she should do, but at the same time she finally knew she wanted a change. She was ready to get away from filming reality shows.

She watched as he drew in a harsh breath. The little moan she'd heard from his lips was sexy as hell. It was getting harder and harder to not jump him, especially when she knew he felt the same way about her. She glanced at his manhood, prominently displayed between his legs as he knelt there. She winced. It looked uncomfortable.

"Are you staying here tonight?" she shyly asked.

"Ah, love, there's nothing I'd like more, but if I do, I think we both know what'll happen. I want you more than you know, but I also want our coming together to be because we know it's a permanent thing. I'll wait for you to know for sure. I don't want to just be an itch you want to scratch. But I warn you now, when you do come to me, I'm keeping you. I won't let you go. When that's what you want, come to me. I'll spend hours making sure you don't regret your decision."

Holy crap. Kina squirmed on the bed. That was hot. She knew when they did finally get together they'd be explosive.

She watched as Jonathan leaned toward her to take her lips with his. He plundered her mouth; there was no other word for it. He tasted and caressed every part of her. It was over long before Kina was ready. He leaned back and put his hand on her cheek. "Thank you for not letting this be the end of us. I'll see you in the morning."

Dazed, Kina could only nod. He was dangerous, that was for sure.

Chapter 14

Kina tried not to laugh, as Darius, Roger, and Nash were fitted with crampons. Their last challenge to determine who the final two contestants would be was a classic Alaskan rite-of-passage. They would be trekking across the Portage Glacier, hitting checkpoints along the way. Of course since the men would be trekking across the glacier, that meant the camera crew would too.

Eddie had actually gone all out and hired a local sightseeing company to fly a helicopter overhead and film the men walking along. Taylor, the lucky duck, was chosen to be the one who'd film from the air.

The men would be, of course, timed,and whoever was the slowest to get to the final checkpoint would be leaving the show. To up the ante, and the drama, the men would be leaving at different times, so they'd have no idea how long the others were taking.

They'd seemed to collect themselves after the last challenge and they all seemed as if they actually wanted to be there again. Kina had been worried after Benedict had left. It would certainly be a let-down of the entire show, if all three contenders bagged the last few competitions. She wasn't sure what had happened to make them change their minds, but the days they'd spent together in the house waiting for the next competition obviously did them good.

Kina wasn't looking forward to the day. She was in

good shape, but knew it'd be tedious and somewhat dangerous to walk on the glacier while filming at the same time. She would have to watch where she was putting her feet, but she couldn't do that with one eye glued to the viewfinder of a camera.

She was assigned to Roger for the day. She actually didn't really have a preference for one man over another. They were all pretty decent guys, the strip club incident notwithstanding. She glanced over at Jonathan. He'd be with Darius for the day. Darius didn't look too sure about having Jonathan following him all day, but she knew he'd get over it as soon as he started concentrating on completing the challenge.

Jonathan had held her hand the entire trip to the glacier. Before they'd gotten out of the van he'd leaned over and whispered in her ear. "Stay safe today, hon."

She got goose bumps every time he'd said that to her. He wasn't just saying it; it was obvious he meant it.

She and Roger were second to start the competition. Carl and Nash were first, and Jonathan and Darius were the last to leave. The trek across the glacier wasn't too strenuous, but there were some large crevasses they had to get around. At each checkpoint the men had to do an activity. At one stop they had to prepare a fish for eating, including scaling it and taking out the guts. At another stop, they were to braid a series of ropes together that could be used in rappelling. And at the last stop, they were supposed to build a sort of snow shelter that would be the type used if they were ever caught out in a snowstorm. For the last activity, Eddie had flown in truckloads of snow to use. The glacier just didn't have the snow needed, on the surface, for that kind of task.

Roger did pretty well at all three of the check points. They were well on their way to the finish line when he stupidly got too close to the edge of a large crevasse. Because of the summer heat and the melting, of the top layer of ice all summer, it wasn't stable. Kina saw the ice start to break off under his feet, before he even felt it.

"Look out!" she called out, not even thinking about keeping quiet for the sake of the show.

Roger whipped his head around to look at her and she could see the second he figured out what was happening. The panicked look on his face spurred her into action. She dropped the camera, without a care to its value, and leaped toward Roger. Luckily he threw his body at her at the same time. She landed on her butt and grabbed his wrists with her hands. She dug her crampons into the layer of ice just at the side of the gaping hole widening under Roger alarmingly.

Roger was kicking at the empty air beneath his legs as he frantically tried to get back to more stable ground.

"Dig your shoes into the ice!" Kina called to him trying to back herself, and Roger, away from the hole. "Do it!" she commanded, seeing he was losing it and panicking. Thank God she had the little spikes on her boots. They allowed her to grip the ice and give them some leverage. Without them, they'd both have been on their way to the bottom of the big crack in the ice by now.

She sighed in relief when she saw Roger listening to her and doing as she said. She was strong, but Roger was a big man, and he was wearing a large backpack which was weighing him down. She wasn't going to let go. She couldn't.

Kina strained backward at the same time Roger tried to use his legs and feet to gain purchase and push himself toward her. Just as she felt her hands slipping off his wrists she felt them slowly making progress. Inch by precious inch they backed away from the cold gaping hole that had tried to swallow Roger. When they'd scooted far enough away that his feet were no longer dangling into space, Kina finally let go of the death grip she'd had on his wrists and watched as he scrambled to his hands and knees and crawled away from the hole in the glacier.

She quickly crab-walked backward at the same time and scooted on her butt to a safe distance away from the unstable ground. When they were both well away from the danger of being sucked back into the hole, they collapsed on the ground.

"Holy shit," Kina said under her breath. "That was close."

She was totally unprepared for Roger to surge upward, grab her hand, and pull her into a huge bear hug. She knew how he felt. She'd felt the same way in Australia when Sam saved her from the poisonous snake. When you see your life pass before your eyes, you're just so grateful to have another chance at living.

"Jesus," Roger exclaimed. "Thank you. Shit." He couldn't seem to form a coherent sentence.

Kina smiled and held him just as tightly. She had to admit to herself that she was probably just as freaked as he was. She patted him on the back, trying to help both of them regain their equilibrium. Finally pulling herself back together, she asked, "You ready to get off this godforsaken piece of ice?"

Roger pulled back and looked Kina in the eyes, not ready to let it go yet. "Seriously, thank you. I don't know what I would've…"

Kina interrupted him. "I know, Roger, I know. I'm glad I was here. You're okay. Let's go?"

They both picked themselves up off the ice and headed toward the finish line. The camera she'd so carelessly dropped as Roger had started being sucked into the hole miraculously seemed to be all right. Kina noticed Roger was being a lot more careful about where he walked. He also kept his pace slow and steady, so Kina could easily keep up with him.

As expected, Carl and Nash were already at the finish point when they arrived, but that didn't necessarily mean they'd been faster than Roger and herself. Since they'd left in waves, there was no telling whose time was faster. Kina didn't say anything about what happened to her and Roger; she just went over to where Carl was standing and joined him. Not too much later, Jonathan and Darius arrived. Jonathan looked relieved to see her as he came into the finish line area. Kina felt the same relief at seeing him. She understood a bit more about why he felt the way he did about her, because she felt that same protectiveness toward him.

It finally struck her. If she felt that way about him, his feeling that same protectiveness about her couldn't be wrong. She knew he wouldn't want her to protect him, but the feeling was still there. It made sense. She got it. Finally. He'd protect her, just as she'd protect him. Knowing what had happened to her and not knowing whether Jonathan was all right as he trekked across the dangerous ice made it all too clear. It wasn't like she wanted to hold him back, or own him; she just wanted to make sure he was safe.

Shannel got the men all lined up the way she wanted and began the ceremony. She went around to each man and talked about their experiences on the glacier. Kina tensed, knowing what was coming. She wished Roger would keep his mouth shut, but knew he wouldn't. His feelings of gratitude were still too raw and new.

"I almost died out there today," Roger said solemnly. It was almost comical how everyone's head whipped toward him as he spoke. Kina kept her eyes on Roger through her lens. She couldn't look at Jonathan right now, finally understanding how he'd be feeling. She knew she'd feel the same way, if Nash dropped a bomb like the one Roger just lobbed into the group.

Of course Shannel encouraged Roger to keep talking.

Roger told everyone how he'd been admiring the bright blue color of the glacier inside the crevasse and how, before he even knew something was wrong, it was collapsing under him. He described how Kina had grabbed hold of him and prevented him from falling to his death. Without lifting her head from her camera, Kina felt Jonathan's hand at the small of her back. He pressed into her, but didn't say anything or further distract her from her job.

Roger embellished the telling of the dramatic story, but the underlying emotion was real. She really had saved his life. She knew it, he knew it, and now everyone else knew it too. Kina watched as Roger broke out of his place in line and started toward her. Jonathan lifted the camera out of her hands, she briefly saw the emotion in his eyes, and then Roger was there. He brought her into his arms and just hugged her, again, grabbing on tight. The retelling of the story had obviously made him emotional again.

Kina closed her eyes and leaned against him. He was a decent guy who'd had the scare of his life. She felt happy; he was man enough to show emotion and not care who was watching. She had no idea if this would show up on TV, knowing how Eddie felt about the contestants mixing with the camera crew, but she didn't care. She was glad she'd been there at just the right time.

When Roger had himself under control, he pulled back and kissed her on the cheek and made his way back toward the other men and Shannel. Kina cleared her throat and reached for her camera, which was still in Jonathan's hands. She risked looking up at him, not knowing what his reaction would be. She had no idea if he'd be pissed or upset or what.

She watched as he leaned toward her and said in a low voice. "I'm so proud of you, Kina. If this wasn't going to be shown to millions of people right now, I'd kiss the hell out of you."

Kina blushed and couldn't say anything. Wow. Just wow.

She picked up the camera and filmed the rest of the ceremony. Nothing remotely as exciting as what happened to Roger had gone on with the other two contestants. They had funny stories to tell about braiding the rope and on trying to get the scales off of the fish. When Shannel finally read off the times for each of the contestants, Kina wasn't surprised to hear that Roger had the slowest time overall.

Roger didn't seem to mind either. His final words for the show said it all. "Even though I'm leaving the show today, I'm leaving with my life, so I feel like I've won anyway."

Because they were on a glacier, Roger couldn't leave the same way the other contestants had. They all had to hike off the glacier to get to the van. Jonathan didn't even flinch, which Kina appreciated more than she could say, when Roger took hold of her hand and held it the entire way back to the van. They didn't exchange any more words about what had happened up on the glacier, but Kina knew they'd created a bond that would never fade.

Kina thought about how close she and Sam were, and understood what Roger was feeling. She could feel Jonathan walking close behind her, keeping watch over her and it warmed her heart. He was letting Roger hold her hand, but she was still aware of him. It was like he'd warned, even though another man had her attention and was close to her, she knew he was there, knew she was his and his alone.

Kina exchanged contact information with Roger before he left the production house. She knew she'd always keep in touch. It was like the old Chinese proverb, if you saved someone's life, it was yours forever. She didn't even startle when she felt a hand curl around the back of her neck. Jonathan. She'd missed that.

"Are you all right, hon?" He seemed to know how emotional she was over what had happened. "You want to talk about it?"

"I'm good." At his skeptical look, she turned toward him and looked up. "I swear, I'm okay."

She fell even more for the man standing in front of her, when he simply nodded. He pulled her toward him and gathered her close. She loved when he did that. It made her feel so cared for, so safe, so loved. Whoa. She didn't want to go there, not yet.

"Would you rather spend a month alone with your lover in a cabin high in the mountains surrounded by snow, or on a deserted tropical island?"

Kina laughed and didn't take her head from his chest as she answered, "If that was an invitation, my answer is that it doesn't matter as long as we're together."

Chapter 15

This was it! The final competition for the show was here at last. Kina knew everyone was ready for it to be over. The weather had gotten colder and the daylight was getting shorter and shorter. Kina had the utmost respect for anyone who chose to live in Alaska year-round. She knew it was beautiful in the summer, with the long summer light and the mild weather, but staying there all-year-long took a special kind of person. She knew she couldn't do it.

Darius and Nash also seemed ready to be done with the show. They were nervous about what they'd have to do for the final competition, but ready to be done with it. Kina didn't think either really cared if he was named the 'Extreme Alaskan', but it was more that they wanted to get home to their own space and friends and family again.

She and Jonathan had worked out an easy camaraderie. They hadn't spent the night together again, knowing what it would lead to if they did. Kina wanted to make love to Jonathan more and more each day, but she also loved that they were taking it slow. It was great getting to know him without the pressure of being naked thrown in.

They did spend the evenings in each other's arms watching TV or just hanging out with the others. They shared some scorching kisses, but tried to keep it at that. They both knew the end of the show meant some decisions would have to be made.

Kina still hadn't decided what to do. On one hand, she wanted to be with Jonathan, but she was honestly scared to death to think about giving up her job. She hated not being able to make a decision one way or another. She didn't want to be a camera operator for reality shows anymore, but she did want to stay in the business. She didn't know how that would work if she moved to Arizona to be with Jonathan. If she started at a new television station, she knew she'd have to start at the bottom and work her way up again, and that definitely didn't appeal to her.

She knew Taylor and Carl were ready to go home as well. They'd started talking more and more about their adorable little girls and she knew they missed their spouses as well. Taylor had been with his partner, Chris, for over fifteen years and Carl had been married to his wife for ten. While they understood the life of a camera operator meant a lot of time away from home, it was never easy.

Eddie had worked hard to make sure the final competition between the two men would be dramatic. He'd chosen to have another overnight adventure, but this time it would be on Bear Island. Bear Island was located southwest of Anchorage in the Katmai National Park and Preserve. It was an actual island on Kukaklek Lake. The best, and quickest, way to get to it from Anchorage was by helicopter.

The island was known to have a large population of brown bears, it wasn't so far from the mainland that the bears couldn't easily swim to it. They found the island to be a perfect place to nest and raise their young. Part of the reason was because the food was plentiful and the predators few. The brown bears had mostly been stuffing themselves with food during the summer, but the danger of an attack was never really gone. The men, and subsequently the camera operators, would have to constantly be on the alert for the massive animals.

Native Alaskans knew to keep clear of the bears, especially this time of year. They were unpredictable and many people were killed each year from bear attacks. Because it was so dangerous, Eddie brought in an Alaskan ranger to talk with both the camera operators and the contestants to go over some basic bear safety.

Kina listened intently as the ranger explained how brown bears were able to run in short bursts up to forty miles an hour and they were also very good swimmers. Darius and Roger were both given bear boxes, which were bear-resistant containers and they were instructed to put any leftover food in, to string up in trees to prevent the bears from entering the campsite after smelling food.

Basically, the ranger told everyone that bears don't like being surprised, they should never be crowded, and they're always looking for something to eat. Kina looked around and saw everyone was paying close attention to the ranger. They all knew Bear Island could be dangerous and they wanted to stay safe.

Kina muffled her laughter when Jonathan leaned over and asked quietly in her ear, "Would you rather be mauled by a hungry bear or a hungry lion?" She shivered as he nipped her ear quickly before facing the ranger again and pretending he hadn't just made her quiver and wish those teeth were nipping somewhere else.

The plan was to drop off the two contestants with two camera operators filming each man on either side of the island. They weren't supposed to interact with each other, but Eddie and the production crew would be stationed on another part of the island. As long as they kept their interactions with each other off camera, it wouldn't be an issue. Each pair of camera operators would have a radio for safety purposes.

The contestants would spend another two nights on the island, in much the same time frame as their last overnight contest. They'd be dropped off around noon today and picked up around the same time on the third day. This time the difference was that each man wasn't given anything to eat, it would be up to them to find their own food. They were to make their own shelter, find their own food, and generally just survive while out on their own. They were given one match, one fishing hook and they were allowed to dress as warm as they'd like.

Kina didn't know what the actual competition was from Eddie's brief explanation, and obviously the men were confused as well. Most of the activities in the past had been based on time or some other type of quantifiable outcome. Finally, Eddie got to the point.

"In order to win and be called the 'Extreme Alaskan', you'll be judged by one of the local rangers. Whichever of you is deemed to have the best campsite, will win. The ranger has a checklist of things she is going to use to see if your site is deemed 'Alaska-worthy.' She'll check to make sure your shelter is solid, you have a good food supply, you have a good place for your fire, etc. We can't tell you all of the criteria. It's up to you to figure out how to make your site a place you, or anyone else, could actually survive in if they were there for a long period of time. Use what you've learned over the course of the last weeks and what you know from your previous experiences. Be safe, have fun, and we'll see you in a few days."

Eddie broke everyone up into their groups. Kina wasn't surprised she and Jonathan were together again. While she was a bit embarrassed, she was also glad. Obviously Eddie wasn't dumb, and after his talk with Jonathan about Jeff, he'd obviously figured out they were together. He could've been a jerk and separated them deliberately, but he hadn't. Another surprise.

Taylor and Carl winked at Kina as they set off with Nash. Kina would've been happy being with either of the other men; luckily, they all got along extremely well, especially now that Jeff was no longer with them.

Kina and Jonathan set off after Darius. He was given instructions on how to get where he was to set up his camp. It started out as a quiet trek because Darius didn't have another contestant to talk to, but remembering what the ranger had said about bears and how they didn't like to be surprised, he started to whistle while he walked. Making noise was a great way to let bears know you were there so they could keep their distance.

Kina would've loved to have been able to make some noise of her own. She was a bit paranoid about the whole bear thing. She had no desire to run into a bear in her lifetime. But since the cameras would pick up any extra noise they made, both she and Jonathan had to keep silent.

After a forty-five minute walk, they arrived at Darius' spot on the other side of the island. It was breathtaking. They were looking south over Kukaklek Lake and the sun was hitting the lake and glistening off it like a million diamonds sparkling on the water. It was beautiful. Kina thought if it was only about fifty degrees warmer, it could almost be a tropical paradise and a place she'd like to come to. Almost.

Darius got right to work. Kina almost felt sorry for him. As a chemist, he hadn't had too much need to run around the woods collecting firewood and trying set up a camp according to some obscure standards he'd be judged by.

Jonathan leaned over and tapped Kina on the shoulder. She stopped filming so he could talk to her.

"Do you want to set up our camp, or continue to film Darius?"

Kina smiled.

"What are you smiling for?" Jonathan asked running his index finger down her cheek lightly.

"Because you asked me which I'd rather do," Kina answered honestly, loving his hands on her. "Most men would've just assumed they'd have to put up the tent while I filmed."

Ignoring her sexist comment, Jonathan instead chose to concentrate on two words she'd said. "*The* tent? We did bring two, you know."

"I know," Kina said blushing. "You can set up the tent; I'll follow Darius for a while."

Jonathan looked around to see where Darius had gone. He was across the clearing, not paying any attention to them, instead he was trying to set up a lean-to with some branches. Jonathan hooked his hand behind Kina's neck and pulled her toward him.

Kina loved that it seemed to be his favorite way to bring her toward him for a kiss. His palm on the back of her neck was like an instant aphrodisiac for her. Her brain knew what was coming and she was instantly ready for him. The kiss, as usual, was intense. It was way too short for Kina's liking, but they both knew they were working and had no time to make out like two horny teenagers.

Stepping back from her, Jonathan said, “Okay, I’ll set up our tent. You follow Darius, but be safe.”

Nodding, Kina headed toward Darius to get some good close-up shots of him setting up his camp.

The rest of the day went by relatively smoothly. Darius managed to get his lean-to set up and miraculously, he was able to start a fire. Kina almost laughed out loud at the victory dance he did after he got it to a safe level. Watching him hoop and holler and skip around the area was just too funny. Kina thought once again how great his actions would be for television. He also managed to catch a small fish in the lake. He didn’t have to worry about any leftovers because he ate the entire thing. She was actually pretty impressed at how well he’d done. She knew she wouldn’t have been half as successful as he was. Thank God, she was filming and not on the show itself.

After Jonathan and Kina ate and the sun went down, it was still way too early to head to bed. They’d gotten some good nighttime shots of Darius lying under his shelter gazing up at the sky and other generic nighttime shots that could be edited into the show wherever Eddie would like to put them in. Both Jonathan and Kina were more than happy to sit around the fire Darius had built and relax for a bit.

They’d all gotten to know each other pretty well over the last weeks, not to mention the recent drama with the strip club, so they were all comfortable hanging out for a while. Kina was going to start the ‘Would you Rather’ game, but then decided she liked that being just between her and Jonathan.

They sat around and talked about nothing important, just the weather, what Darius had planned for the next day and what he’d do when the show was over.

"Maybe after the show airs, you'll be so famous some hot chick will look you up."

Kina and Darius laughed at Jonathan. Kina picked up where Jonathan left off.

"Yeah, even though this wasn't a dating show, it could still work out for you."

Darius laughed. "I'll just be glad to go back to my nice, plain, boring life. I think I'll tell anyone who'll listen to not apply to be on a reality show. It's not all it's cracked up to be."

They all laughed. After about two hours or so, Jonathan stood up.

"Thanks for letting us share your fire, Darius. We're going to hit the sack. We'll see you bright and early in the morning."

Darius nodded at them and didn't even make any comments about the two of them having only one tent set up. Kina figured after Jonathan's 'talk' with him there was no way he'd chance being disrespectful in any way toward her. It was obvious they were 'together' and Darius didn't seem to have any issues with it.

Climbing into the tent felt awkward this time around. The last time they were on site outside it seemed more natural. Kina figured it was because there was more sexual tension in the air now and they were more aware of each other.

She settled down on the sleeping bag Jonathan had put down and waited for him to join her. Jonathan had taken the ranger's words to heart and had put their MREs inside the bear-proof container and strung it up over a tree about fifty yards away. He didn't want to take any chances of a bear wandering into their tent looking for food. That was one of the most dangerous situations people could get into with a bear. The ranger told everyone several horror stories about campers who'd either been in their tent when a bear got curious, or who'd gone into their tent, believing it would protect them from a bear. There was nothing to do but fight if that happened. Kina didn't want to have a fight a bear in such close quarters as this little tent.

Jonathan zipped up the door flap and shut off the flashlight, leaving them in total darkness. It was intimate in a way that being in a bed together hadn't been. Kina felt him take off his boots and then strip off his jeans. She sighed as he gathered her into his arms and drew the second sleeping bag over them. God, she loved being in his arms like this.

After a moment of silence Jonathan said softly, "I've missed this."

Kina had too, but they both knew why they hadn't been sleeping in the same bed. It was the big hairy gorilla in the room they'd both been ignoring. He'd said he wanted them to get to know each other before making love, but he'd also said he wanted to wait until she was ready to give herself to him. To be with him. He wanted her to be able to say with one hundred percent conviction that she wanted to be with him.

"I've missed it too," was all she could say in response.

Jonathan didn't let the subject drop as Kina hoped he would.

"Have you thought anymore about coming to Arizona with me, once this show is over?"

Kina shifted in his arms until she rested her chin on his chest. She could just make out his face. As much as she wished they didn't have to have this conversation, she knew it was time. Hell, it was past time to have it. "I've thought about it," she hedged, still not knowing what she'd tell him.

"What's holding you back, hon?" Jonathan asked tenderly. "Talk it though with me, let me help you, ease your fears."

"But you'll find reasons for me to move, no matter what I say," Kina said in frustration. "How can I talk it through with you when I know you'll try to convince me to move down there no matter what reasons I come up with for not wanting to?"

Jonathan was silent for a long while. Kina turned back on her side and rested her head on his shoulder again, keeping her arm thrown over his rock-hard abdomen.

"I want you with me, Kina," he finally said. "I want you with me more than anything. I'd do just about anything to get you there with me, for you to want to be there with me. But I don't want you to agree and then regret it later. I want you to move to Arizona and be *sure* it's where you want to be. I could tell you the streets were lined with gold there and I know you'd still only come when you're ready."

Kina chuckled. It seemed like he did know her after all.

"I love you, Kina." Jonathan threw it out there like a grenade. It sat between them, scary and exciting at the same time.

After hearing no response from her Jonathan continued. "I want you to know. Just as I told you earlier, you're mine, and I want to make sure you know how I felt. I'm not asking you to move and change your entire life on a whim. You're it for me. Period. If you want to do the long-distance thing for a while, I'll do it, but know I ultimately want you with me. In my house. In my bed. You're the one for me. You're my *One*. I want to marry you. Spend the rest of my life with you."

Kina started to panic. She wasn't ready for this. She hadn't known Jonathan long enough. She tensed.

Jonathan ran his hand over the small of her back soothingly. "Don't freak, hon. God, I wasn't going to go there tonight, but I don't know how else to make sure you know I'm serious. I'm not some young college kid who wants a one-night-stand. I want you. Just you. All of you. But only when you're ready."

Kina was still silent. She couldn't get any words out. On the one hand she wanted to immediately say yes to whatever he suggested, but the more logical and stubborn part of her was screaming at her to slow down, that this couldn't be real.

Jonathan kissed her forehead gently and kept his lips on her skin. She could hear him breathe in deeply, as if inhaling her essence into his soul. "Shhhh, just relax, love. No pressure. Let's get through the rest of this show and then we can talk again if you need to. I won't bring it up again, but I'm not sorry I told you how I felt. Sleep now. I'm right here, I'm not going anywhere."

Chapter 16

Kina came awake slowly the next morning. It was still dark, as the sun rose much later in the morning than she was used to. She lay still and enjoyed being in Jonathan's arms. They were in much the same position as they had been when they fell asleep; there wasn't much room in the tent for much moving around anyway. He was on his back with his arm around her waist and she was using his shoulder as her pillow and was on her side with one arm curved over his stomach. Kina heard his light snoring as he breathed in and out. She moved her head a fraction and took in a deep breath. God, he smelled good.

Oh she knew most people probably wouldn't agree, after all they'd spent the day hiking and working, and then part of the night in front of a smoky camp fire, but those smells intermingled with his natural scent was heady. He smelled strong, like he could conquer mountains and slay dragons. She wished she could wake every morning with his smell in her nostrils.

Kina paused. Hell. She could, if only she was brave enough. Ultimately, that was what it came down to. Was she brave enough to take the leap and trust Jonathan? She was scared. It was a frightening thought to think about leaving what she knew, her career, and leaping off a cliff into the unknown. But she knew Jonathan would be there for her. He was her parachute. So, what was holding her back? Why wasn't she jumping at the chance to be with him?

It was because of her past. She hadn't had good luck with relationships and she was terrified this would end up the same way, no matter what Jonathan said. She couldn't really remember, but she knew she'd probably thought she felt the same way about Matt before she moved in with him too. She tightened her arm around Jonathan and snuggled deeper into his side.

She felt him stir and clasp her to him as he woke.

"Good morning, love," he said sleepily. "What time is it?"

"I have no idea."

"Have you been up long?"

Kina shook her head. "No, just lying here enjoying being in your arms." She decided to be honest with him.

Jonathan gave her another squeeze and kissed the top of her head. "I haven't had any nightmares in a while," he said unexpectedly.

Kina raised her head. "What?"

"I haven't had any nightmares since we talked," he repeated. "I heard what you said about it not being my fault. I even called Dean one night and had a long talk with him. I told him how I was feeling and he reacted the same way you did. I took your words to heart and decided to believe you." Jonathan laid it all out there, holding nothing back.

"Thank God," Kina said fervently. "It wasn't your fault. You're so protective with me; I know you were the same with Becky."

"Thank you, Kina. Thank you for believing in me and helping me get through that."

Kina blindly raised her mouth to his, not thinking for a second about morning breath or what she might smell like, only needing to feel his lips and tongue on hers. Jonathan obliged her and devoured her mouth with his. Soon, that wouldn't be enough, but for now, here, it was perfect.

They slowly made their way out of the tent and into the chilly morning air. Darius was already awake and sitting next to the fire. He'd most likely not slept that well and that was why he was up already. Kina wandered off to do her morning ablutions and Jonathan wandered in the opposite direction. They met back at the tent and gobbled down a quick MRE. They didn't want to flaunt their food in front of Darius, but they had to eat to have the energy to haul their cameras around all day and to keep up with whatever Darius had planned for the day.

Darius spent most of the morning fishing. He remembered the ranger saying they had to have enough food to last for a while, so instead of worrying about berries and other grasses he could collect, he concentrated on getting protein.

Overall, he was a very good fisherman. He seemed to have mastered the art of using the hook he'd been given. He' tied it to a long thin stick using some of the flexible weeds that grew around the shore. He walked out into the lake a little ways and was very patient. He'd either gotten used to the cold water or he was numb. Either way, he'd captured some little crawfish that were along the shore to use as bait and had stood in the water for a long while catching fish.

Kina watched as the pile of fish on the shore grew. She glanced at Jonathan nervously. She put her camera down and waited until Jonathan noticed and had done the same.

"Do you think that's okay?" she said pointing at the

pile of fish lying on the rocks. She was worried about bears. Would they smell the fish and think it was a free lunch?

"I have no idea." Jonathan answered, looking around. "What if we move over there?" He pointed at a rock sticking out a bit over the water, away from where Darius was fishing.

Kina nodded in agreement. She was all for getting away from anything that might attract a bear. "Should we say something?"

"Normally, I'd say no, we aren't supposed to interfere with the show, but I think this is a safety issue."

Kina agreed and Jonathan called to Darius to let him know their concerns. The other man called back that he was almost done and would come into shore and deal with the fish in a moment.

Jonathan and Kina moved to the rock and continued filming. They watched as Darius caught another fish and moved toward the shore. He waved at them, letting them know he was done. Jonathan helped Kina off the rock and they both moved toward Darius.

Kina froze. Holy crap. Her worst nightmare was coming true. A brown bear was ambling down the shore right toward Darius. Without thinking she grabbed Jonathan's arm and yelled out at Darius.

"Darius! Behind you!"

He turned and as soon as he saw the bear, he forgot everything he'd learned from the ranger. He dropped the makeshift fishing pole and the fish he was carrying and turned and ran straight for them.

The bear, used to chasing his prey, immediately roared and gave chase. Darius ran past them as fast as he could. Jonathan grabbed Kina and held her in place.

"Don't run, Kina," he warned.

Kina *couldn't* run. She was frozen in place. The bear stopped ten feet from the two of them. It stood on all fours and swung its head from side to side. Kina heard it clacking its teeth together as if practicing biting down on their tender flesh.

"Spread your arms out," Jonathan said, not trying to lower his voice. "Make yourself appear as big as possible."

Kina did as Jonathan instructed. Neither one had thought to drop their cameras. She watched as the bear stood there, still swinging its head and opening and closing its mouth. Crap. She had no idea what that meant in bear language, but it couldn't be good.

"Now, start walking backward," Jonathan continued to instruct. Kina noticed he kept himself between her and the bear. No, no, no, no. This wasn't happening. She suddenly remembered all the times Jonathan had told her how he'd protect her and stand in front of her, if necessary. She'd never been so scared in all her life. She was scared for herself, of course, but she was also scared for Jonathan.

The bear didn't seem impressed with them at all. It made a growling noise and followed them as they backed up. Suddenly the bear was done playing nice. The smell of the fish and Darius running had obviously made all of its protective instincts kick in.

It came at them suddenly and before Kina could do anything, it took a swipe at Jonathan. He still had his camera in his hand and used it to block the blow. A swipe from a bear could kill an elk or deer with one blow, so Kina knew Jonathan was in big trouble. The camera went flying from his hand and landed with a thud fifteen feet away. That was way too close. Thank God it hit the camera and not Jonathan. Kina had leaned forward to hand her camera to Jonathan for extra protection when the bear came at them again.

Jonathan saw Kina lean forward at the same time he saw the bear's paw come toward them again. He didn't have anything else in his hands to protect her with so he simply pushed her backward with one strong shove on her chest and stepped into the space she'd just been standing in. The bear's paw struck him right across the lower stomach. It would've hit Kina in the chest had she still been standing there. Jonathan fell to the ground without a sound, clutching his stomach.

Shit. That hurt. Jonathan looked around frantically. He was on the ground now, not a good place to be when confronted by a brown bear. Brown bears were part of the grizzly family and he knew he had very little time to do something to save both himself and Kina. He grabbed a handful of dirt and rocks from next to him and threw it at the bear as it came toward him again.

He heard Kina yelling at the bear and frantically trying to talk to him at the same time. He couldn't answer her; he was concentrating on the bear coming right for him. Suddenly, Kina's camera was dropped in his lap. He grunted with the pain of it landing on the wounds from the bear but he grabbed it and held it up just as the bear went to hit him again.

Once again the bear's claws hit the camera and it went flying.

Adrenaline flowing through his body, Jonathan crab-walked backward as fast as his abused body would let him, still trying to grab handfuls of the loose sand and throwing it at the bear's head. He saw sticks flying from behind him as well. Kina was still there, throwing whatever she could get her hands on to try to get the bear to retreat.

"Get the hell out of here, Kina!" he yelled at her, hoping like hell she'd follow his instructions.

No way!" she yelled back, continuing to throw things at the bear.

Finally, as the two of them backed toward the trees, the bear stopped following them. It stood there and growled and clacked its teeth together as Kina tried to pull Jonathan's arm to help him move back out of its way. Jonathan gritted his teeth. He was in severe pain. He knew it was bad, but he had to get them away from the bear in case it decided to charge them again.

After they'd moved about twenty feet away, the bear turned around and headed toward the pile of fish Darius had left on the ground. Jonathan could feel Kina trying to pull him upright. He used all his strength, and most of hers as well, to climb to his feet and stumble along beside her. He had no idea where she was taking them, but as long as it was away from that damn bear, he was happy.

Kina dragged Jonathan along beside her as far as her strength would allow. Jonathan was practically dead weight way before she got back to the camp. They weren't going to make it back to the tent and the first aid kit they'd brought along. She eased him to the ground, looking around nervously. She looked down at Jonathan. He'd lain down on his back and had his eyes closed. Kina took a closer look. Oh, shit. His shirt and hands were covered in blood.

Kina reached down, noticing her hand shaking uncontrollably, and lifted the bottom of Jonathan's shirt. After taking a look she quickly dropped it and pressed her hands hard to his stomach. She ignored his inhalation of pain at her actions. She tried not to throw up. She concentrated on breathing in through her mouth and out through her nose. She thought she'd seen what might have been his intestines. He was hurt. Bad. She had to get him help.

"Darius!" She screamed into the still forest. She couldn't leave Jonathan because she was literally holding his life in her hands. "Darius!" She yelled again. He'd better still be around. God, what if that bear smelled Jonathan's blood and came back for more? What if there were other bears around. She had no idea how that worked, but fresh blood in the forest couldn't be good. Crap. Crap. Crap.

"Would you rather…" Kina heard Jonathan say in a breathy voice, "…be mauled by a bear… or a lion?" Kina saw him smile weakly. "I'm thinking neither, at this point." He answered his own question.

"Shut up, Jonathan. Just be quiet. You're going to be fine. Just fine." Kina sniffed, desperately trying to keep herself under control. Crying wasn't going to help Jonathan at this point.

Jonathan hurt. He knew it wasn't good. "No guilt, love, promise me."

Kina shook her head in denial. She knew what he was doing. "No, just no. You shut up. You're going to be fine. *Darius*!" She screamed one more time. Where the hell was he? She needed him. Now.

Jonathan laid his hand over hers lying on his ripped-open stomach. He couldn't look down, but could feel it was bad. "Love, remember what I said. I'd do anything to protect you. Anything. I'm glad it was me."

Kina's eyes filled with tears again. Shit. She hadn't believed him. She knew he said he loved her but this was too much. No one had ever done anything like what he'd done for her today. Her father hadn't even wanted her born. Her high school boyfriend didn't respect her and Matt had just wanted to own her. She knew he never would've given his life for hers. "I never asked for you to do this," she said brokenly, not being able to stop the tears coursing down her face and dripping onto their joined hands over his stomach.

"That's what love is. Not having to ask."

Kina watched as Jonathan's eyes closed and his hand went lax and fell off of hers. *No. This wasn't happening.*

Darius finally came running through the woods toward her. She had to get help.

"Kneel down here and put your hands where mine are," she ordered curtly, once again gaining control over her riotous emotions.

"What happened?" Darius asked.

"What the hell do you think happened?" Kina snapped. "He was mauled by a bear. The same damn bear you ran from and led right to us." Darius had no response. "I have to run back to camp and get the radio. He needs help. Whatever you do, don't let go. Keep the pressure on his stomach. I don't care if that bear comes back. You. Do. Not. Move. Got it?"

At his nod Kina lifted her arms and waited until Darius had a good strong grip on Jonathan. Before running off, she leaned down and kissed Jonathan's lips. "I'll be right back, don't die on me," she whispered and then was gone through the trees.

Kina ran as fast as she could back to the camp and snatched up the radio. She frantically radioed the production camp and explained between harsh breaths that Jonathan was badly hurt and they needed a helicopter. Eddie hadn't wanted to believe her until she cussed him out and threatened a lawsuit if he didn't get someone out there soon.

Eddie obviously had planned for some sort of emergency care in case someone needed it, because within twenty minutes, a helicopter was landing on the same shore Darius had been fishing at and where the bear had attacked them. Kina had taken over holding Jonathan together while Darius went to meet the chopper at the lake. He led the paramedics back to the forest where Kina was kneeling on the ground. They took one look at the amount of blood on her hands and on the ground underneath Jonathan and packed him up and got him on the stretcher and headed toward the helicopter. They didn't spend any time trying to put in an IV in while they were in the wilderness. They just packaged him up and were on their way.

There was no room in the chopper for Kina so she could only watch as Jonathan was taken away. He'd never regained consciousness. Left with Darius in the clearing, the silence was heavy. They could no longer hear the *whoop whoop whoop* of the helicopter as it sped toward Anchorage.

"I…" Darius started to say and stopped as Kina's hand came up.

"No." Kina said as she started gathering up the pieces of the ruined camera equipment strewn about the area. She had to get to the hospital, but she still had a job to do. The attack ran through her mind like a record spinning over and over. Picking up the pieces of equipment was like picking up pieces of Jonathan.

She got everything back to camp and radioed Eddie. He was pulling Carl off of Nash's campsite and sending him to hers. He'd take over the rest of the filming so she could get to the hospital and Jonathan. Kina shouldn't have been surprised that Eddie wasn't going to stop the show, but she was. Why she'd thought his camera crew meant more than the show, was beyond her.

After all her back and forth with herself about whether she should quit or not was not, it a moot issue. She was done. So done. There were times during the filming she'd thought maybe Eddie was changing and perhaps she'd sign up to continue to work with him. But now there was no way in hell.

Carl gave her a big hug when he got to her campsite. Kina noticed there were two rangers carrying shotguns who arrived with him. At least Eddie had sent along extra security. At least she wouldn't have to worry about the rest of them out at the lake while she was with Jonathan at the hospital.

She didn't say a word as she sat in the helicopter Eddie had to arrange to take her to the hospital. He'd made a token protest at the cost of flying her back separately from the rest of the crew, but quickly shut his mouth at her ferocious words threatening all sorts of lawsuits.

As soon as they landed at the Anchorage airfield, Kina took out her cell phone. Thank God she finally had service. The first thing she did was call Dean, Jonathan's brother. She didn't have his parents' numbers, but Jonathan had programmed his brother's number into her phone for emergencies. She supposed this was definitely an emergency.

"Hello?" Dean answered after the first ring.

Kina got right to the point. "Dean, this is Kina, I'm working with Jonathan in Alaska. There's been an accident. Jonathan's in the hospital."

Kina could hear him moving around quickly. "What happened?"

"He was swiped by a bear. I have no idea how bad

it is, but I think it's *bad*. They flew him off the set and to the hospital here in Anchorage. I'm on my way there now, but I don't know anything." Her voice cracked. "I don't know if they'll talk to me since I'm not related to him, so you'll want to get here as soon as you can."

"I'm on my way, Kina. I'll call the hospital and give them permission to talk to you. Keep me up-to-date. I don't know how long it'll take me to get there."

"Do you want me to call your parents?" Kina asked, hoping like hell he'd say no.

"I'll take care of it. You just get to my brother. If you talk to him, tell him we're on our way."

Kina agreed and hung up. Thank God Dean would be there soon. She flagged down a taxi and headed to the hospital.

* * *

Kina stood off to the side of the waiting room. The last twenty-four hours had been the longest she'd ever experienced in her life. Dean had arrived, as had the rest of Jonathan's family. Becky, his mom and dad, and even some of the people who worked on the refuge, she'd recognized them from the shoot they'd done there. They all showed up to support their son, friend, and brother.

Kina felt completely out of place, but she couldn't go anywhere until she knew Jonathan was going to be all right. The doctors had come out periodically to update the family on his condition. They'd explained the extensive injuries Jonathan had and how the bear's claws had actually perforated his bowel as they'd swiped across his abdomen. They'd gotten him sewed up, but their main concern now was infection. Not only were the bear's claws covered in bacteria and dirty as hell, the waste material from his bowels had leaked into his body as well, so it was a double whammy.

Jonathan was fighting as hard as he could, but it was just a matter of time to see if he'd pull through. Kina teared up. God, now she understood more what Jonathan had been talking about when he'd talked about his feelings of guilt when it came to Becky. The one nap Kina had managed to squeeze in, ended abruptly with her jerking awake because she'd been reliving the exact moment Jonathan stepped in front of her to take the bear's swipe. Guilt. It was an insidious emotion. Nothing anyone could say would assuage it.

She thought back to their brief moment in the woods before he'd passed out. Jonathan had tried to tell her not to feel guilty. He knew she would. She knew he'd be pissed at her for feeling this way and she tried really hard to tamp it down.

Jonathan's mom, Bethany, came toward Kina. His mom was the last person Kina wanted to talk to. She just knew the eagle-eyed woman would take one look at her and know this was all her fault. So she was completely shocked when the older woman walked right up to her and folded her into her embrace. Kina couldn't help it; she'd been strong for so long, but that one little bit of sympathy broke her. She burst into tears and buried her face in the other woman's hair and just cried.

When she finally came back to awareness she noticed she was sitting on a small couch in the waiting area with Bethany still holding on to her tightly.

"I'm so sorry," Kina said, pulling back to wipe at her face.

"What are you sorry about? You looked like you really needed that; both the shoulder to cry on and the cry itself."

"Well yeah, I just cried all over you and you don't even know me!" Kina said, shocked this woman would even want to take the time to comfort someone who was basically a stranger.

"I know you. And even if I didn't, you're Jonathan's *One*. That means you're family."

"Wh-what?" How did she know that? Had he talked to his mom about her?

Bethany sighed. "Has he told you about our family?"

"Uh, yeah." Kina drew out the word in confusion. She thought she knew where Bethany was going with this and it was a bit awkward.

Bethany didn't take offense, but instead just smiled.

"So, he did tell you, but you don't really believe it. Let me tell you a story, Kina. In my family," Bethany gestured behind her at her husband and other son, "the men have one woman who is meant to be theirs. One. They go through life knowing this, but not really believing it until they meet her. It happened with Robert, my husband. He was going on his merry way, saving lives, then boom! He met me at the scene of an accident and knew I was his one and only love. Dean was the same way. He was a ladies' man. Never settling down because it never felt right. Then he met Becky. Obviously you know their story. It wasn't easy, but Becky was his *One*. This has happened over and over throughout our family history. We have story after story of our ancestors who never thought they'd get married, never thought they'd find that one person who completes them, until one day they did. The same thing happened with Jonathan. He hadn't really talked to you on the set until he went to all of the crew to see if any of you could help Becky. He talked to you and knew. Kina, you're his *One*."

Kina was shocked and confused. Jonathan *had* told her he loved her and had told her the story of her being his *One*, but she'd pretty much blown him off, thinking he was just being romantic. She couldn't understand how Jonathan's mom knew about her, though.

Bethany must have seen her confusion. She took hold of Kina's hand and held it tightly. "He told us, dear. As soon as he came back to the house after meeting you, he came bursting in the room and said 'I've found her!' He's been wooing you. It can be a hard thing to hear and believe. It sounds crazy, but I see you already knew some of this already. He trusted you enough to tell you."

Kina looked up from their clasped hands to see Becky and Dean standing in front of them. She turned and saw Robert, Jonathan's dad, standing to the side, watching his wife carefully.

"It's true, Kina," Becky said softly. "I know it sounds crazy, but the Baker men would do anything for their *One*. I know you're feeling guilt about what happened to Jonathan, but, stop it right now. Seriously. He's been through this too and I've told him over and over that I don't blame him nor do I want him to blame himself. You haven't told us what happened out there and how he came to be hurt exactly, but we can guess. He was probably protecting you, right? Somehow he was hurt instead of you."

Kina looked down at her hands. God, hearing it out loud was so much worse than thinking it in her head.

Dean took over for his wife. Kina noticed the protective hand he had at Becky's back and how she was curled into his side. "We're protective. It's in our genes. Jonathan isn't quite as alpha as I am, but if you were in trouble, or Becky, or our mom, or really any other woman, he'd do anything in his power to protect you. I can imagine you were filming and a bear came up on you. He probably stood in front of you and took that bear on."

"Close enough." Kina mumbled, completely floored by what this family was saying.

Dean went on. "He loves you, Kina. You're his *One*. He'd do anything for you, just as I suspect you'd do for him. Don't feel guilty. Put yourself in his shoes. God forbid it was you lying in that bed, would you want him to feel guilty for you protecting him?"

Kina sat up straight on the couch. Oh crap. Dean was right. He was so right. That was just what she needed to hear to give her a kick in the pants. She'd be pissed if the tables were turned and Jonathan was feeling guilt about her getting hurt while protecting him. She'd been telling him over and over about how she could take care of herself, and now, look. Loving someone, having someone love you, wasn't about being independent and moving through life on your own, it was about protecting each other. Being there for each other when needed. She'd helped Jonathan through some hefty guilt he'd been feeling just as he'd helped her with that damn bear. She had to get her act together.

Kina stood up and hugged Dean as hard as she could. Of course she couldn't even get her arms all the way around him, he was so big. He uncurled his arms from around Becky and held Kina tight for just a moment. He put her away from him and looked into her eyes. "You're okay, now?"

"I'm great." Kina said with steel in her voice. She had things to do and people to talk to. She'd make this right, once and for all.

* * *

Jonathan gradually became more and more lucid over the next couple of days. It wasn't until his third day in the hospital that he was awake enough to recognize anyone. Dean happened to be in the room when he came to.

Because he still had a breathing tube in, he couldn't talk. He was agitated and Dean saw the panic in his eyes. He put a hand on his brother's forehead and one on his chest. He leaned down to speak into his ear. "Settle, bro. You're fine. Kina's fine. You're in the hospital, but you're healing and we'll get that tube out of your throat so you can talk, all right?"

Jonathan looked up and saw the honesty in his brother's eyes. He wouldn't lie to him. Dean knew what Kina meant to him. He *knew*. Jonathan relaxed and closed his eyes. He'd believe his brother, but he still wanted to see Kina.

Two days later, Jonathan was leaving the hospital and he still hadn't seen Kina. She'd disappeared. He heard all about his mom's conversation with her, but no one had spoken with her. It was if she'd vanished into thin air. It was killing him. He'd let her run for now, but he'd find her. He wasn't giving up on her. He couldn't. He needed her.

He pushed the hurt down. He was hurt she hadn't come to see him in the hospital. Surely, after everything they'd been through, she'd want to make sure he was going to be all right. He tried to put himself in her shoes. She was scared and feeling guilty. She probably thought she was being noble or something and thought leaving him was the best thing she could do for him. Well, screw that. He'd make sure she knew how much she meant to him. As soon as he got back on his feet, he'd find her and somehow make her understand how much he loved her. She had to. Without her, he was nothing.

Dean and his dad had arranged for him to get home via a chartered plane. Jonathan knew it had to cost a whack, but he also knew he'd never make it if he had to fly commercial. He'd argued to stay in Anchorage and recuperate, but his family wasn't having any of it. The only reason he wanted to stay in Alaska was Kina. He thought maybe if he stayed there, she'd come see him and let him convince her she was his world.

The doctors signed all the papers and put him in the care of his family. Dean and Becky drove him to the airport so he could lie down in the back seat, and his parents took a taxi. The few friends who had flown up when he was first hurt had already left a few days ago. They'd headed back to Arizona to make sure the refuge was taken care of. Jonathan was wheeled onto the plane and settled himself into the cot that had been set up for him. He was quiet. All he could think about was leaving Alaska and Kina. Where was she? Was she all right?

The plane ride was uneventful and soon they were on their way to his parents' animal refuge and home. He hadn't had time to find a place to live yet. He'd been planning on doing that after the show as over, and hopefully with Kina. He wanted to find a home she'd feel comfortable in.

After the long trip Jonathan finally gave in and took a pain pill. He was in quite a lot of pain and only wanted to sleep. That was a lie, he only wanted Kina, but after that he wanted to close his eyes and let the fog of the pain medicine take him. As he settled into the queen bed in his parents' guest room, he felt someone at his side. He cracked his eyelids open, hoping against hope it was

Kina. It wasn't.

Becky sat down at Jonathan's bedside and took his hand in hers.

"You'll find her when you're better." She knew.

Jonathan took a deep breath. "What did she say to you, Beck? Do you know where she went?"

Becky shook her head. "I don't know, but I have a feeling she'll find her way to you. She was dealing with some pretty heavy stuff in the hospital. She was feeling guilty you were hurt protecting her." At Jonathan's shake of his head she hurried on. "We told her she shouldn't feel guilty. I even hinted to her that she'd do the same thing if the tables were turned."

"Did she get that?" Jonathan asked, tortured by the thoughts of Kina feeling bad for one second about what he'd done. He hated the thought of Kina being the one hurt and lying in a hospital room, but he knew she'd protect him in a heartbeat if she had to.

"I think she did. She got a weird look on her face and ran out of the waiting room like a fire had been lit under her. She loves you, Jonathan. I'd bet my life on it. You should've seen her. She was magnificent. She got hold of us and helped arrange for all of us to get to the hospital. She kept us informed about what was going on with you until we could get there. I know you don't remember this, but at one point the doctors weren't sure they wanted to do surgery because you were so weak. She knew if they didn't do it, there was a high chance you wouldn't survive. From what the doctor told us, she browbeat them into agreeing it was the only thing to be done, and you were in surgery before we even arrived."

Jonathan smiled weakly. He could imagine Kina doing just that. "I can't keep my eyes open, but tomorrow I'm going to find her."

Becky smiled. She had no doubt he'd do just that.

* * *

Kina sighed. The last two weeks had been so frustrating. She'd gone back to the production house intending to talk to one of the producers, but she'd forgotten no one was there, they were all still on Bear Island. She had no way to get out there, and honestly didn't want to. She had way too many bad memories to want to ever lay eyes on it again.

She had to wait another two days for Eddie and the others to get back. Taylor and Carl wanted to know how Jonathan was. Since she hadn't been back to the hospital she could only say that he'd be fine. She didn't know the particulars, but was thankful Dean had been texting her and keeping her in the loop.

Dean was the only person in Jonathan's family who knew what she was planning. She hadn't wanted to tell anyone other than Jonathan, but she also wanted to make sure at least one member of his family knew she was coming back. She wasn't deserting him. She just had some things to take care of first.

Kina sat down and met with Eddie. The meeting was a long one, but after it was over Kina knew her life had changed, hopefully for the better. She'd taken a risk. She hoped, but wasn't one hundred percent sure, that Jonathan would think what she'd done was a positive thing. Only time would tell.

Before sitting down with Eddie, she'd had a long talk on the phone with Dean. She didn't want to go behind Jonathan's back, but she had to secure her future before she could involve him. She knew he'd do whatever it took to get her to Arizona, and she appreciated it, but she had to do this on her own. For her to feel any feeling of accomplishment, she had to make this happen herself.

Dean, at first, wasn't too sure about having anything to do with Eddie. He'd never gotten over what had happened to Becky, and Eddie wasn't on his list of favorite people. After talking it over with Becky and having his lawyers look over the paperwork she'd faxed to him, he'd finally agreed. Kina smiled, remembering how he'd told her in a disgusted voice, "I'm only agreeing because you're family." Family. Maybe she'd finally get the loving family she'd always dreamed of.

It was time to get to Arizona and to Jonathan. She'd heard from Dean that Jonathan had been snarky and grumpy and downright annoying. God, she missed him and hated like hell that she hadn't been able to talk to him, but it was time to face him and let him know what she'd done. She only hoped he still wanted her in Arizona with him.

Ironically, she was at the airport at the same time as Darius and Roger. She hadn't seen Darius since that day on the island and she was honestly glad to be able to say good-bye to him. A little bit of her was still pissed at him for his role in what had happened to Jonathan, but after she'd thought about it for a while, she realized she probably would've run the same way he had. If Jonathan hadn't been there with her, telling her to calm down and stay still, she probably would have taken off right after Darius. She had to forgive him for being too scared to think straight.

They were all on separate flights, making their way home, but managed to have time to sit down for a drink before they had to leave.

After giving Darius a big hug and telling both men

all about what had happened to Jonathan and how he was recuperating in Arizona with his family, she couldn't resist asking which one of them won the show and now had the title of 'Extreme Alaskan.' She couldn't believe it when neither would tell her!

"You'll have to watch the show with the rest of America, Kina," Darius had teased. "You know we're under contract to keep silent."

"You mean after everything we've been through together, you're seriously not going to tell me?" Kina asked, annoyed. "You owe me!"

Both men laughed at her.

"Consider this payback for all those horrible shots you took of us," Roger told her, only half-kidding.

Kina got over her snit quickly, because honestly she didn't really care who'd won in the long run. She gave each of the men another big hug before heading off to her gate. "Thanks for being pretty cool about everything," she told them. "I've been on shows with some pretty horrible people, and you guys are all right."

They knew she was teasing and told her they'd see her later.

Kina knew they wouldn't, but it was a nice sentiment.

A few hours later Kina's nerves were getting the better of her. She was more nervous at what would happen next than she'd been for her first job interview as a camera operator. Dean had assured her Jonathan wanted her with him, but until she saw that for herself firsthand, she just wasn't sure.

After getting the rental car, Kina checked the map on her cell phone for the tenth time. She couldn't believe she was just going to show up at the refuge where Jonathan was staying with his parents, but she just wanted to get it over with. She couldn't go another day without seeing for herself, that Jonathan was alive and well. She could still remember the feel of his warm blood seeping through her fingers, as she frantically put pressure on his stomach, while they were in the woods on the island.

Every now and then she'd have a nightmare where he'd be walking toward her holding his intestines in his hands, and asking 'why.' She shivered. Yeah, it was time to see him for herself and make sure he was okay.

Jonathan was sitting at the dining room table talking with his mom and making a list of places to start looking for Kina when the doorbell rang. Bethany got up and went around the corner to the front door. Jonathan didn't get up, he still wasn't moving very quickly these days and he was concentrating on his list.

He heard the surprise in his mom's voice when she opened the door, but couldn't hear her actual conversation with whoever was at the door. He steeled himself to entertain another one of his parents' friends. They'd been coming by at regular intervals to check on him. It was annoying, but sweet at the same time.

Jonathan couldn't believe his eyes when his mom returned with Kina in tow. He was stunned. He'd been all ready to set off to find her and here she was!

Jonathan slowly stood up and held himself steady with one hand on the tabletop. He simply stared at his *One,* as she stood in the doorway.

Neither noticed as Bethany disappeared into the back of the house.

Kina shuffled her feet. God, He looked like crap, but so good. He was standing in front of her, alive, and whole. Not knowing how he'd take her being there, she didn't move.

Jonathan had no such hesitation. He stepped toward her unsteadily. He had to have her in his arms right now.

Kina saw him falter as he came toward her and that loosened her feet. She lunged at him and they met halfway across the kitchen. She wrapped her arms around his waist carefully and leaned against him. God. How could she ever have thought for a second about not coming here to be with him? She only felt whole in his arms. She felt his hand come up and cup the back of her neck as he always did. It felt heavenly.

Jonathan let out a shaky sigh. She was here. She'd come. "Thank God," was all he could get out. "Thank God you're here."

Kina nodded and couldn't help the tears that coursed down her face and soaked into his chest. "I wasn't sure you still wanted me to come."

Jonathan drew back and took her chin in his hands. He hated to see her cry, but he had to make sure she understood his next words. "I was making plans to come find you, love. I wanted you to come. I would've spent the rest of my life searching for you so I could convince you to stay with me." When Kina buried her head against his shirt again he couldn't help but tease her. "Would you rather have a beautiful woman wipe snot on you after crying or have her sneeze on you?" She laughed as he meant her to.

Jonathan shuffled with her, still snuggled in his arms, over to the couch. He carefully sat, not jostling his abdomen too much, and settled into the cushions with his *One* in his arms. After she'd stopped crying, he finally asked, "Why'd it take you so long to get to me?"

Kina sat up part way and rubbed her hands over her face. Gah. She knew she had to talk to him, but she wasn't a pretty crier. Some women could cry crocodile tears and not mess up a speck of their makeup, not her. She got blotchy and her eyes swelled up terribly. When she looked up at Jonathan, he was looking at her as if she was the most beautiful woman in the world. God, she loved him. Yes. Loved. Him.

"I love you." She couldn't hold it back anymore. Being here in his arms was a miracle. She hadn't known if she'd ever feel the strength in his arms again. That bear had scared the crap out of her and made her understand just what she had in Jonathan.

"I love you too, Kina."

Kina nodded. "I know." She smiled sheepishly at him. "I should've told you before now, but I was scared. I wasn't sure how you could love me. *Me*. I'm nobody important. I haven't done anything important in my life. No one will remember my name. I didn't understand. Then you got hurt and I was literally holding your life in my hands and I knew. We don't have to do anything, we don't have to be famous, we can just love each other and be happy together. I wanted that. I wanted that more than I wanted my next breath, but you were lying under me and I was holding your intestines in my hands. I was scared to death."

Jonathan interrupted her, "But you did what you had to do, didn't you, love?" Kina nodded. "You did what you had to because you're strong on your own. You don't need me to be strong; you're independent and a hell of a woman. Any other woman might have fallen apart and panicked. You did everything right, Kina. I'm here. I'm alive. You're a hell of a woman. My woman."

Kina smiled. "Hey, this is me talking, not you." Jonathan smiled and nodded as if to say 'go ahead.'

"So there you were, lying unconscious in a hospital bed and I had to bully the doctors into not giving up on you, because I knew deep down, you'd fight. You'd fight to get back to me. And you did. Once I knew you were going to pull through, I had to make it so I could move down here and be with you." At the look in his eyes she hurried on. "I know, I know, I could've quit my job and sat around eating bon-bons and you wouldn't care."

She loved watching him laugh. She didn't love the wince that came along with the laugh, though. Obviously, laughing pulled at his still-tender stomach muscles.

"I went to see Eddie. I had to wait until he'd finished filming on that damn island. Then he gave me hell and negotiated with me for a few days before we could sign our new contract."

Jonathan scowled at her. "New contract? Wait a minute…"

Not letting him continue, she put her hand over his mouth to shut him up. She felt his tongue caressing the palm of her hand and she pulled her hand back. "Don't distract me!" she scolded him, "or I'll never get to tell you."

Jonathan pulled her hand back to his mouth and kissed the palm. "Go on love, I'll be good, but this story had better end with you living here in my house and spending every night in my bed and in my arms, or I won't like it."

Kina shook her head. Every now and then his alpha tendencies would come out. She tried to tell herself it was annoying, but the truth was, she loved it.

"I didn't want to move here and not have anything to do. I actually like being behind a camera and I'm good at it." Kina said the last with no pomposity in her voice. She was a good camera operator and she knew it.

"I talked with Dean…"

Jonathan interrupted her for what seemed like the millionth time. "You talked to Dean? You mean, he knew where you were this entire time?"

Uh-oh. She didn't mean to get Dean in trouble. She tried to hide her smile. Jonathan was so cute. "Uh, yeah, but anyway…" Jonathan growled and pushed Kina backward until she was reclining on the couch. Kina didn't fight him because she wasn't sure how hurt he still was. She giggled.

"I've been going out of my mind trying to figure out how to find you and my brother knew where you were and was actually talking to you this entire time?" Jonathan asked again, in a mock-gruff tone.

"Yeah, but I didn't see you texting me at all. I would've answered."

"Are you kidding me?"

Kina shook her head. She hadn't meant to hide away from him, and she was telling the truth. She would've texted him back in a heartbeat if he'd contacted her.

"Why didn't you text *me*?" Jonathan asked, hurt.

"I wasn't sure whether you were pissed at me or not, and when Dean told me you were all right and not mad at me, I figured it was better if I just came here and talked to you in person. Besides, the more time went by, the more awkward I felt about contacting you out of the blue. I convinced myself you were better off healing on your own and didn't need my issues holding you back."

Jonathan shook his head in amazement. "I can't believe I didn't think to just pick up my phone and shoot you a note. I'm an idiot."

Kina put her hand on his face. "You're my idiot." She leaned up and kissed him briefly on the lips. Before he could deepen it, she pulled away. "Do you want to hear the rest of this or not?"

"Not."

She laughed and pushed at his chest. Jonathan briefly laid his forehead on hers. Then he sighed in mock aggravation. "Okay, okay, please continue. But as I said before, this story had better end with you living here in Arizona with me."

Kina decided to just get it out so they could move on to more pleasant things. "I consulted with Dean and we worked out a deal with Eddie where I'd film documentaries on women who are in need of security, and their stories. I wanted to tell the world about the plight of people who are stalked and to try to see if we couldn't help change the stalking laws in this country. I figured, the more we highlight the personal side of these women, the more people will see they're just regular people who happen to have had the wrong kind of person get obsessed with them. Do you know that in a typical one-year-period there are six point six million people over the age of eighteen who are stalked? And over a lifetime, sixteen percent of women and five percent of men feel they've been a victim of stalking or thought that they, or someone close to them, would be hurt or killed? That's crazy! People are crazy!"

Jonathan could only smile in wonderment at his love. She was so passionate, he was lucky to have found her.

She continued, "And not only that, but I told Dean he needed to look into helping not only women, but men too. Did you know that twenty four percent of stalking victims are men? That's a quarter of all victims! There are crazy women out there terrorizing people too. Women aren't the only victims here!"

Jonathan couldn't stop himself from kissing the hell out of his woman.

Kina was surprised, but quickly joined in with enthusiasm. She'd never take this for granted again. Jonathan's lips were devouring hers and she loved it.

He pulled back and between nips of her luscious lips and asked, "Is there more?"

Kina tried to remember what she'd been talking about. Oh yeah. Stalking, Dean, Eddie, her job. She summed up the rest of her story quickly. "So I have the job of filming you guys as you help out stalking victims and working with Eddie's company to get the documentaries produced and aired."

"And you're here for good?"

"Yes, if you want me."

"I want you."

Kina smiled up at the most handsome man in the world. Her man. If someone had told her a year ago she'd meet the man of her dreams while working, she'd have said they were crazy. Her heart had been as frozen as Alaska was in the winter. She'd never thought she'd meet anyone who could thaw it out and make her love him as much as she loved Jonathan. As she thought back over the last year, she reflected on how she'd almost died in Australia, had spent a crazy couple of months filming a show that would never air, and finally, came face-to-face with a bear and lived. Most importantly, she'd met Jonathan, *her One*.

As she settled back onto the cushions of the couch and reached up to her man, she knew she'd finally found paradise.

Sam, Becky, and Kina sat around the small table in the bar just off the beach and raised their glasses toward each other.

"To life-long friendship!" Becky said a bit too loud. Since this was their tenth toast to nothing in particular, none of the friends seemed to notice the volume of her toast.

"To life-long friendship!" Kina and Sam repeated, then downed their shots.

After moving into their small house, both Jonathan and Kina wasted no time in settling down. Kina didn't think his parents had forgiven them yet for running off to Vegas to get married, but Kina had never dreamed of a big wedding. Truth be told, she never thought she'd ever get married in the first place. So they'd followed Becky and Dean's example and headed off to Nevada. They'd had a quick wedding with just Dean and Becky, and Sam and her husband Alex there as witnesses. It was perfect.

Kina had missed Sam and was happy they were able to at least see each other now and then, but they made sure they kept in touch via weekly phone chats to just catch up.

Kina loved traveling with Jonathan and Dean when they went to help set up security for someone who was being stalked. Dean was true to his word and had started including men in his business as well. He told her he'd honestly not even thought about a man being stalked, but after talking to some of the victims, he'd changed his mind pretty quickly. Women were just as crazy as men, and sometimes even more so, when they were stalking someone.

Kina loved being married to Jonathan. It was inevitable that they'd fight, as they both had such strong personalities, but making up was so much fun.

The first time Kina had seen Jonathan's scars, she'd broken down. She'd traced them over and over with her fingertips and with her mouth, trying to reassure herself he was whole again. They'd had another long talk about guilt afterwards. Kina admitted she'd felt such guilt that he'd been the one who had been hurt when she felt it should've been her. They'd even gone to see the same counselor Becky had seen after she'd been violated, and it seemed to help both of them. The woman had talked them through their feelings and they'd both agreed to let it go. They were both here and alive and together. It was enough for them both.

They'd never found out who was ultimately named the 'Extreme Alaskan.' Their last paycheck arrived in the mail and that was the last either thought about the show. As far as Kina was concerned, Jonathan had more than earned that title all by himself. Her friends were amazed she didn't care who won, but they respected her wishes to not talk about it. All it did was bring back bad memories for Kina. She was way too busy with her documentaries and helping out on the animal refuge to give it any thought, anyway.

The couples' weekend had been thought up by Becky and Kina one night. They'd had a tough week and decided they wanted to get away. Knowing their husbands wouldn't let them go by themselves, they let them come too. Kina thought about Sam and asked if she and Alex could come as well. Becky had agreed wholeheartedly. She'd met them while her reality show was filmed and liked them on sight. Sam had given her some great advice and she was happy to get to know her better.

So now, they were sitting at a bar on the beach, ignoring the looks from the men at nearby tables and drinking themselves silly. They knew their men weren't far away, watching over them. They'd had a conversation once after the last time they'd all gotten together and compared notes. They realized that none of their men ever got drunk when they did. Kina asked Jonathan about it and he'd responded that the guys agreed to let them have their fun and they'd be there to make sure no one harassed them and to keep them out of trouble, if it came to that.

It was overprotective and sweet at the same time. The three women also realized how good the sex was after their nights out. It was as if the men looked forward to them going out simply because of the uninhibited sex that happened afterwards. They'd all laughed and shrugged. They loved their men and loved the long, lovemaking sessions after their nights of drinking just as much.

"I think we should give ourselves a name!" Becky said excitedly. "We all met because of stupid Eddie and his reality shows…let's call ourselves the 'Reality Chicks'!"

"No, the 'Reality Bitches'," Sam said, laughing herself silly, thinking it was the funniest thing ever.

"You guys know what?" Kina said semi-seriously, hammered, but wanting her friends to know how much they meant to her. "We're bound together because of reality shows. That's amazing. I'm so glad I met you all. We're like the six shades of reality."

Kina felt Jonathan's arms around her waist before she could see him. He leaned down and put his cheek against hers. "Having fun, love?" Kina turned and blindly sought his lips with her own. How long had it been since she'd had him? She couldn't remember, but it had to have been too long. The feel of his hand curling around the back of her neck never failed to make her melt.

Alex picked Sam up and sat down on her stool, holding her tight in his arms. She giggled and wrapped one arm around his neck, but kept hold of her drink with the other. She leaned in and latched onto his neck, sucking hard. "Hey! Watch it!" he told her, knowing she'd ignore him. She loved marking him, especially when she was drunk. She always said she had to put her mark on him so no other woman would get any ideas.

Dean turned Becky and stepped into her space. She spread her legs, inviting him to stand between them. He put his forehead against hers and just held her. She was his life and he felt like the luckiest man alive having her in his. He knew how precious life was and how easily it could be taken away.

Kina turned back toward the group. She loved this. She loved all of them. She cleared her throat and raised her glass. She waited until everyone did the same. Becky had to lean over and smack Sam on the back of the head to get her to pay attention. After everyone's giggles died down, Kina said as solemnly as she could, seeing as she was three sheets to the wind, "To reality shows!"

Sam said "Reality Bitches!"

Jonathan added his own toast, "To all of us...friends forever—beyond reality!"

The End

About the Author

Susan Stoker has a heart as big as the state of Texas where she lives, but this all-American girl has also spent the last fourteen years living in Missouri, California, Colorado, and Indiana. She is quite the romantic and even met the love of her life on "Hotmail classified" before online dating and sites like match.com even existed!

Susan has been reading romance novels since middle school and once crossed out the names of the main characters in a book and changed them to her own and to the name of her crush. She's been writing scenes for years, developing her unique writing style.

Susan loves writing but her true passion is adopting dogs from rescue groups and shelters. Susan and her husband have had a total of nine "rescued" dogs since the year 2000, including a variety of basset hounds and bloodhounds. She has recently branched out and adopted a basset/terrier mix who acts more like a terrier than a basset (i.e. digging, eating a couch and being hyper). If you love romance and want to help her support adopting great dogs, be sure to check out her work listed below.

If you enjoyed this book, or any book, please consider leaving a review. It's appreciated by authors more than you'll know.